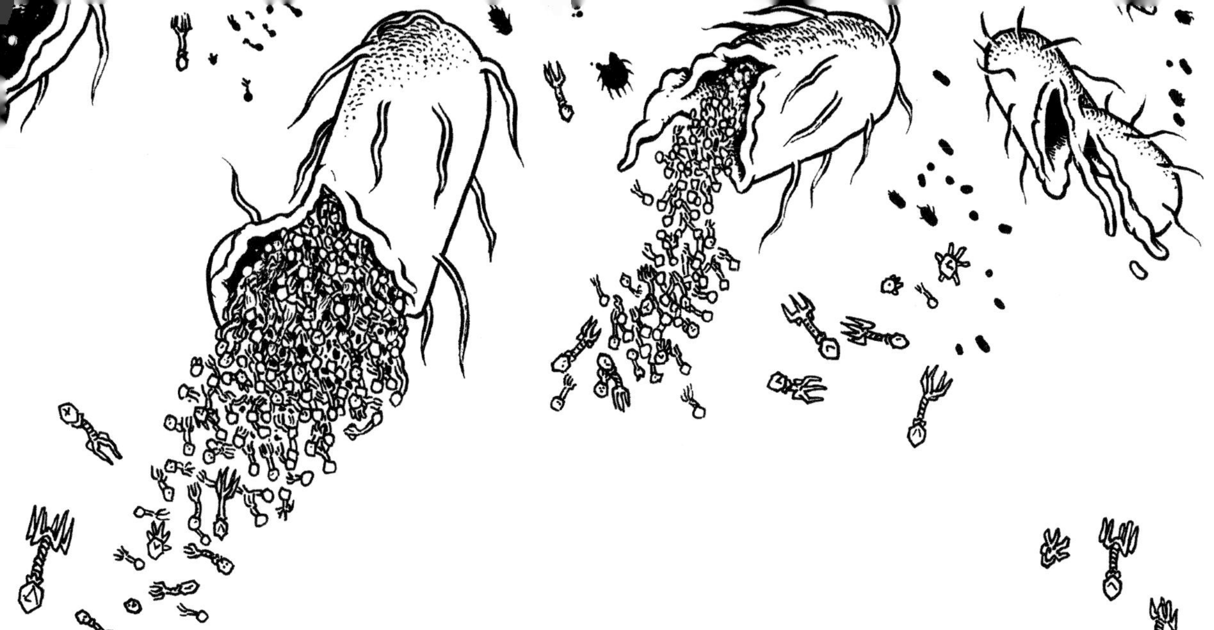

THE INVISIBLE WAR

A WORLD WAR I TALE ON TWO SCALES

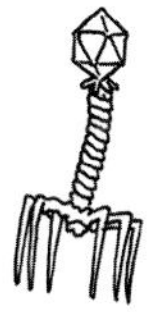

Created by BRIONY BARR & DR. GREGORY CROCETTI
Written by AILSA WILD, in collaboration with DR. JEREMY BARR
Illustrated by BEN HUTCHINGS

Graphic Universe™ • Minneapolis

This story is dedicated to nurses everywhere

Created by Briony Barr and Dr. Gregory Crocetti
Written by Ailsa Wild in collaboration with Dr. Jeremy Barr
Illustrated by Ben Hutchings

First American edition published in 2019 by Graphic Universe™

Published by arrangement with Scale Free Network
The Invisible War: A Tale on Two Scales © by Scale Free Network 2016

Graphic Universe™ is a trademark of Lerner Publishing Group, Inc.

Graphic Universe™
A division of Lerner Publishing Group, Inc.
241 First Avenue North
Minneapolis, MN 55401 USA

For reading levels and more information, look up this title at www.lernerbooks.com.

Library of Congress Cataloging-in-Publication Data

Names: Wild, Ailsa, author. | Barr, Briony, creator. | Crocetti, Gregory, creator. | Barr, Jeremy, author. | Hutchings, Ben, illustrator.
Title: The invisible war : a World War I tale on two scales / created by Briony Barr and Dr. Gregory Crocetti ; written by Ailsa Wild in collaboration with Dr. Jeremy Barr ; illustrated by Ben Hutchings.
Description: First American edition. | Minneapolis : Graphic Universe, 2019. | Originally published: Collingwood, Victoria, Australia : Scale Free Network, 2016. | Summary: In 1916 on the Western Front, Annie Barnaby nurses combat-wounded and sick soldiers, but a smaller and equally deadly battle is occurring in her intestines as her phages fight dysentery.
Identifiers: LCCN 2018019098 (print) | LCCN 2018027871 (ebook) | ISBN 9781541542716 (eb pdf) | ISBN 9781541541559 (lb : alk. paper) | ISBN 9781541545281 (pb : alk. paper)
Subjects: LCSH: Graphic novels. | CYAC: Graphic novels. | Dysentery—Fiction. | Nurses—Fiction. | Human body—Fiction. | World War, 1914–1918—Campaigns—Western Front—Fiction.
Classification: LCC PZ7.7.W546 (ebook) | LCC PZ7.7.W546 Inv 2019 (print) | DDC 741.5/994—dc23

LC record available at https://lccn.loc.gov/2018019098

Manufactured in the United States of America
1-45329-38809-9/10/2018

The creation of the Australian edition of this graphic novel was generously supported by grants from

VICTORIA State Government

ANZAC CENTENARY
–2014–2018–
Sharing Victoria's Stories & Making Connections

Australian Government

Australia Council for the Arts

CREATIVE VICTORIA

creative partnerships australia

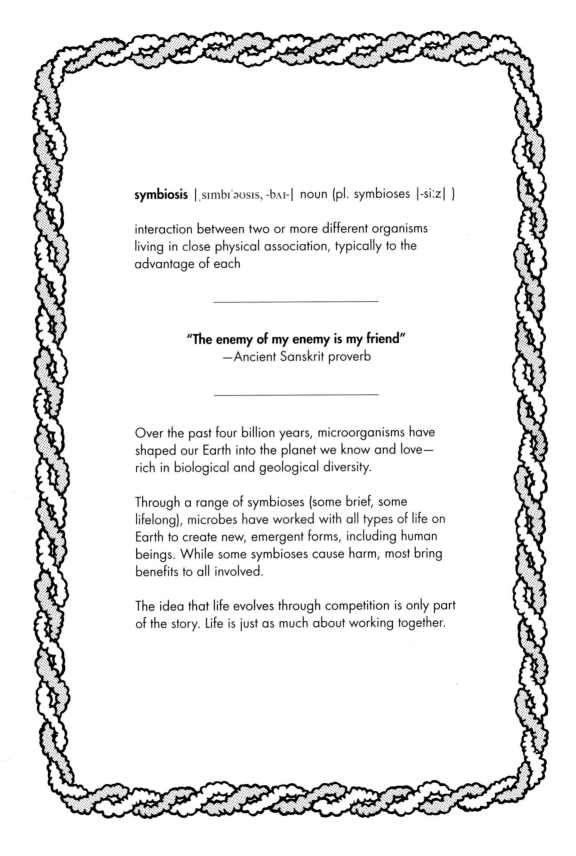

symbiosis |ˌsɪmbɪˈəʊsɪs, -bʌɪ-| noun (pl. symbioses |-siːz|)

interaction between two or more different organisms living in close physical association, typically to the advantage of each

---

"The enemy of my enemy is my friend"
—Ancient Sanskrit proverb

Over the past four billion years, microorganisms have shaped our Earth into the planet we know and love—rich in biological and geological diversity.

Through a range of symbioses (some brief, some lifelong), microbes have worked with all types of life on Earth to create new, emergent forms, including human beings. While some symbioses cause harm, most bring benefits to all involved.

The idea that life evolves through competition is only part of the story. Life is just as much about working together.

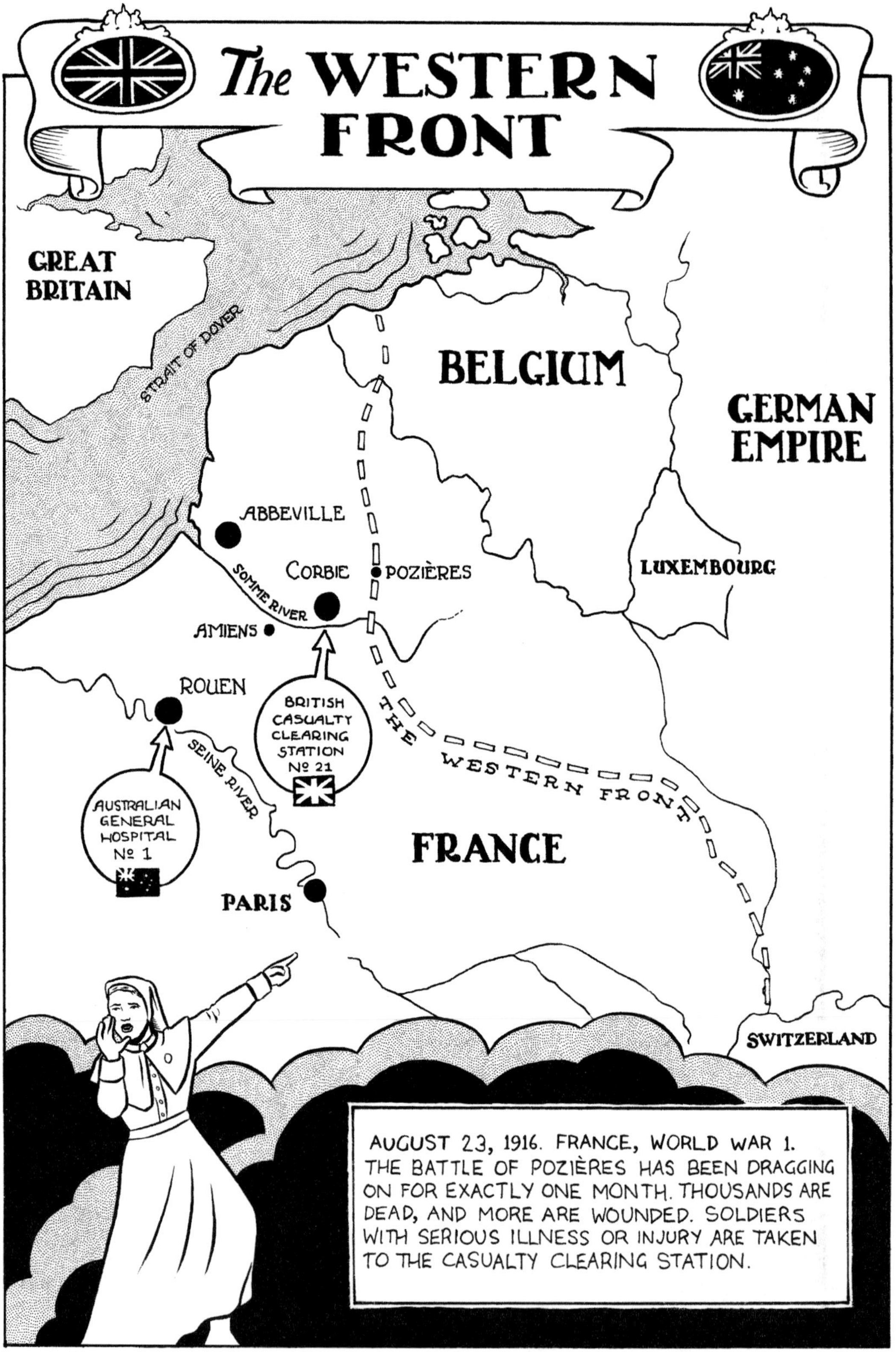
The WESTERN FRONT
GREAT BRITAIN
STRAIT OF DOVER
BELGIUM
GERMAN EMPIRE
ABBEVILLE
CORBIE
POZIÈRES
LUXEMBOURG
SOMME RIVER
AMIENS
ROUEN
BRITISH CASUALTY CLEARING STATION № 21
THE WESTERN FRONT
SEINE RIVER
AUSTRALIAN GENERAL HOSPITAL № 1
FRANCE
PARIS
SWITZERLAND
AUGUST 23, 1916. FRANCE, WORLD WAR 1. THE BATTLE OF POZIÈRES HAS BEEN DRAGGING ON FOR EXACTLY ONE MONTH. THOUSANDS ARE DEAD, AND MORE ARE WOUNDED. SOLDIERS WITH SERIOUS ILLNESS OR INJURY ARE TAKEN TO THE CASUALTY CLEARING STATION.

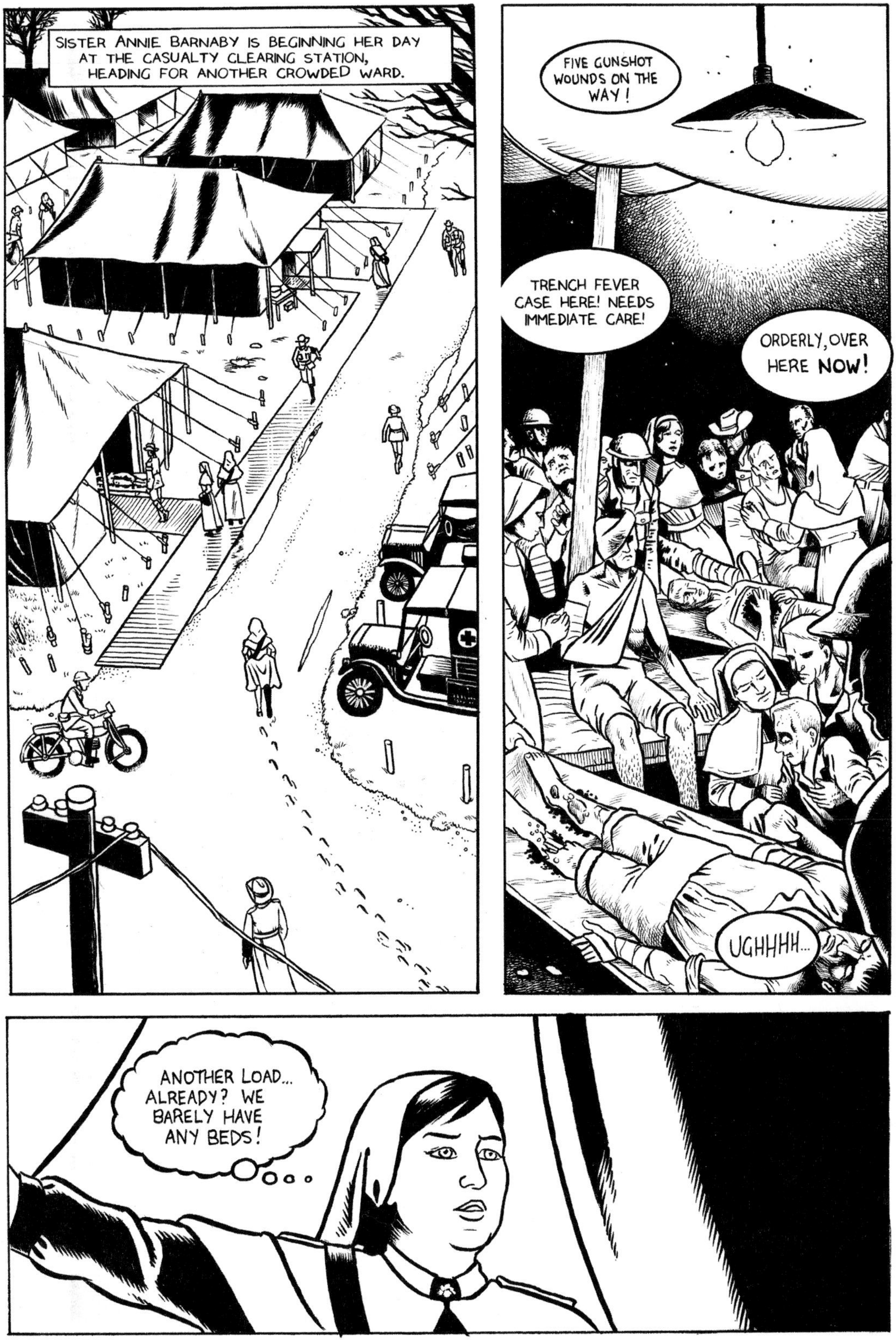
SISTER ANNIE BARNABY IS BEGINNING HER DAY AT THE CASUALTY CLEARING STATION, HEADING FOR ANOTHER CROWDED WARD.
FIVE GUNSHOT WOUNDS ON THE WAY!
TRENCH FEVER CASE HERE! NEEDS IMMEDIATE CARE!
ORDERLY, OVER HERE NOW!
UGHHHH...
ANOTHER LOAD... ALREADY? WE BARELY HAVE ANY BEDS!

ANNIE! THANK GOODNESS YOU'RE HERE. THEY NEED ME IN THE OPERATING THEATER. DID YOU SLEEP?

MAYBE AN HOUR. MORE THAN THESE POOR BOYS.

GET YOURSELF OVER TO SURGERY. I'LL BE FINE.

NOW WHAT'S HAPPENING WITH YOU PRIVATE...

ROBBINS?

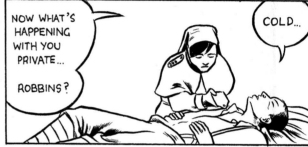

COLD...

Name:
Private
Robbins

Diagnosis:
Diarrhoea

WE HAD TO PACK HIM, SISTER. COULDN'T STOP EVERY FIVE MINUTES FOR HIM TO GO.

POOR BOY, HE LOOKS SO DEHYDRATED.

THEY'VE PACKED HIM WITH FILTHY RAGS. I SUPPOSE THAT'S ALL THEY COULD FIND.

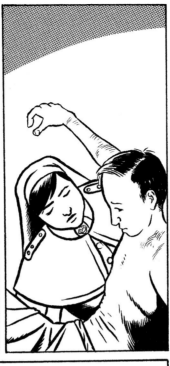

URGH...THESE ARE TOTALLY SOILED...

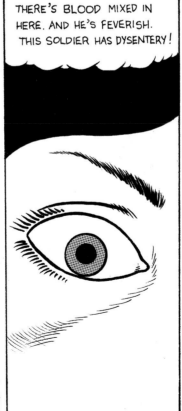

THERE'S BLOOD MIXED IN HERE. AND HE'S FEVERISH. THIS SOLDIER HAS DYSENTERY!

PRIVATE ROBBINS, I'M AFRAID THIS IS MORE SERIOUS THAN A SIMPLE CASE OF DIARRHEA.

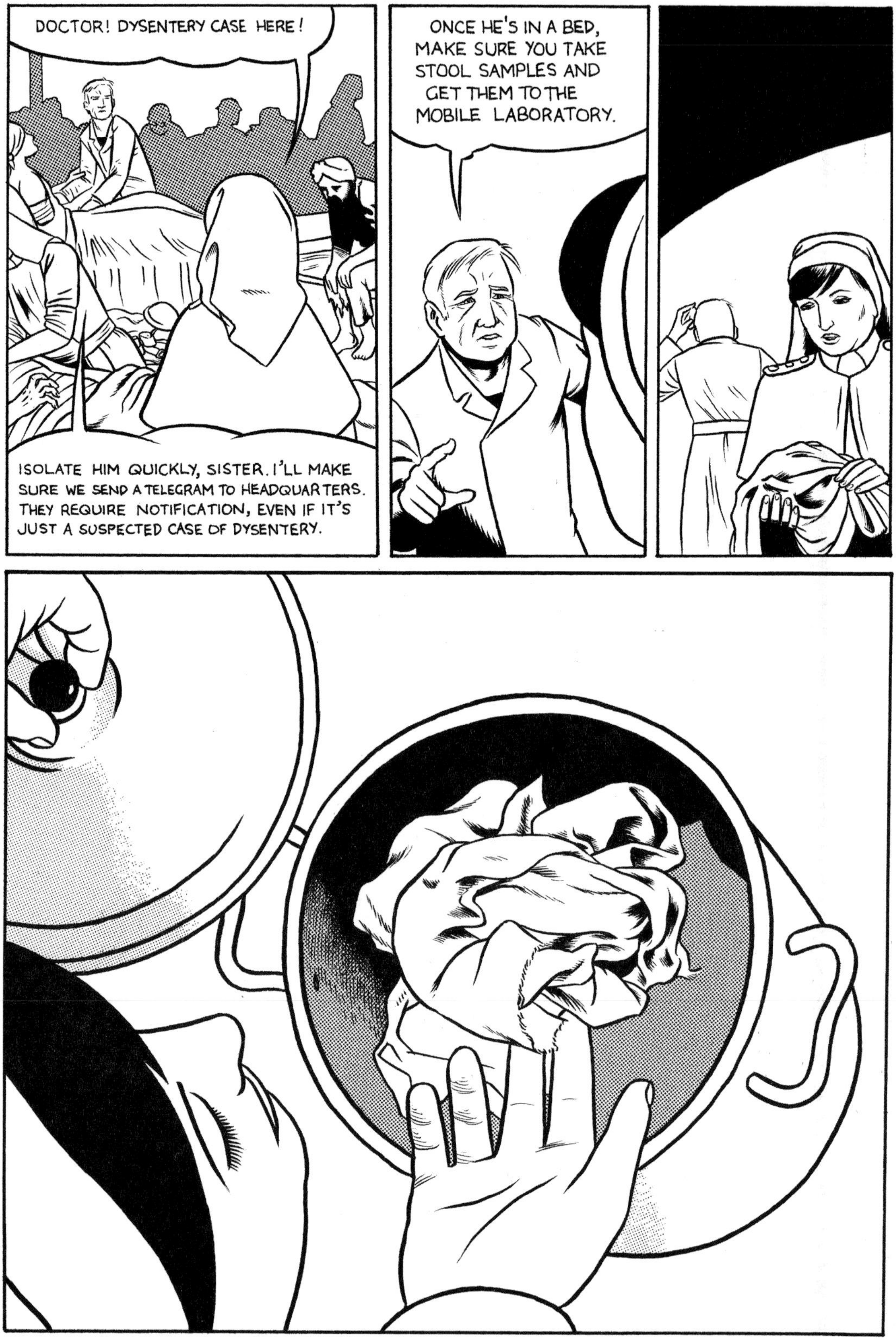
DOCTOR! DYSENTERY CASE HERE!
ISOLATE HIM QUICKLY, SISTER. I'LL MAKE SURE WE SEND A TELEGRAM TO HEADQUARTERS. THEY REQUIRE NOTIFICATION, EVEN IF IT'S JUST A SUSPECTED CASE OF DYSENTERY.
ONCE HE'S IN A BED, MAKE SURE YOU TAKE STOOL SAMPLES AND GET THEM TO THE MOBILE LABORATORY.

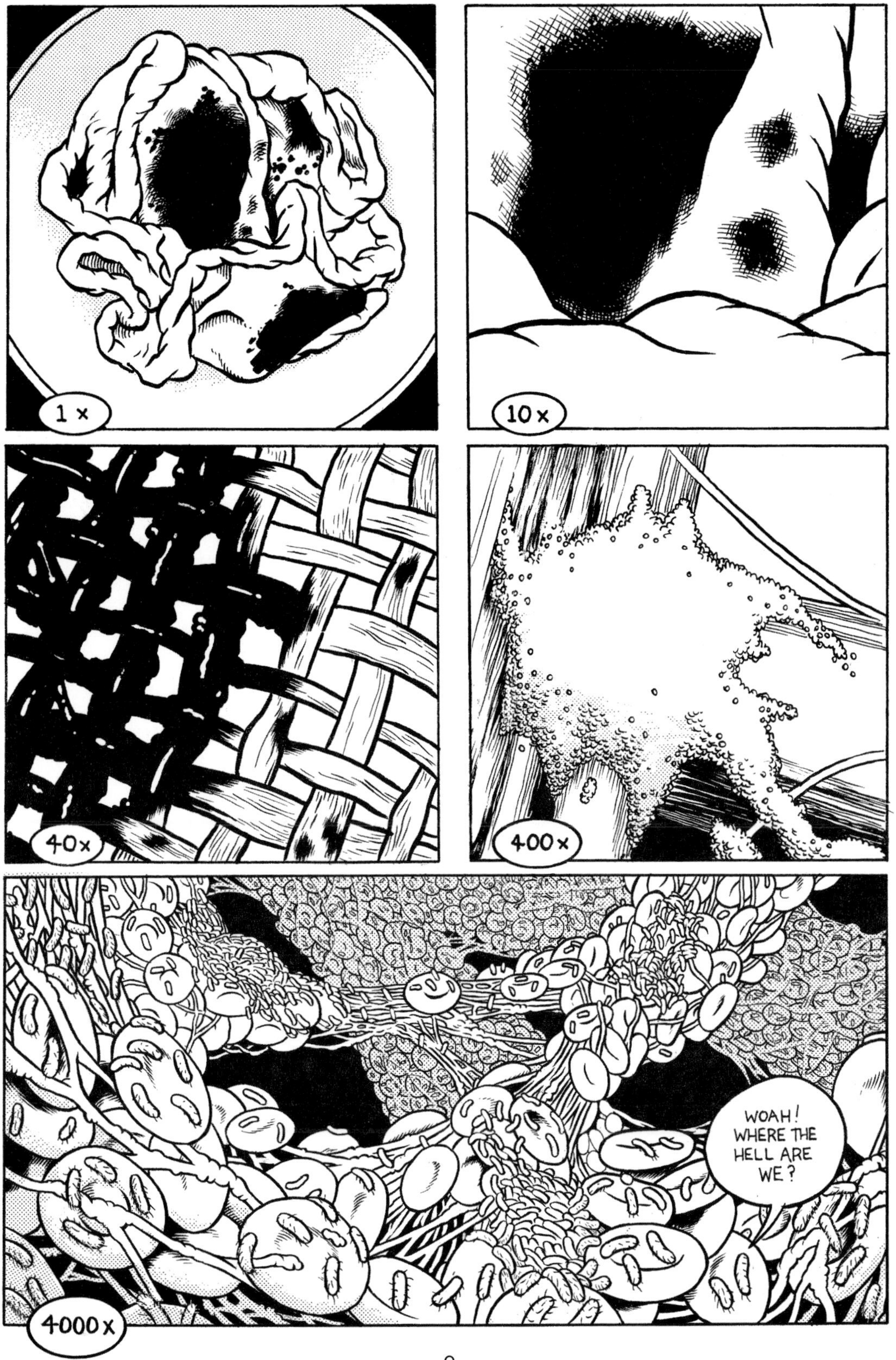
1 x
10 x
40x
400x
4000x
WOAH! WHERE THE HELL ARE WE?

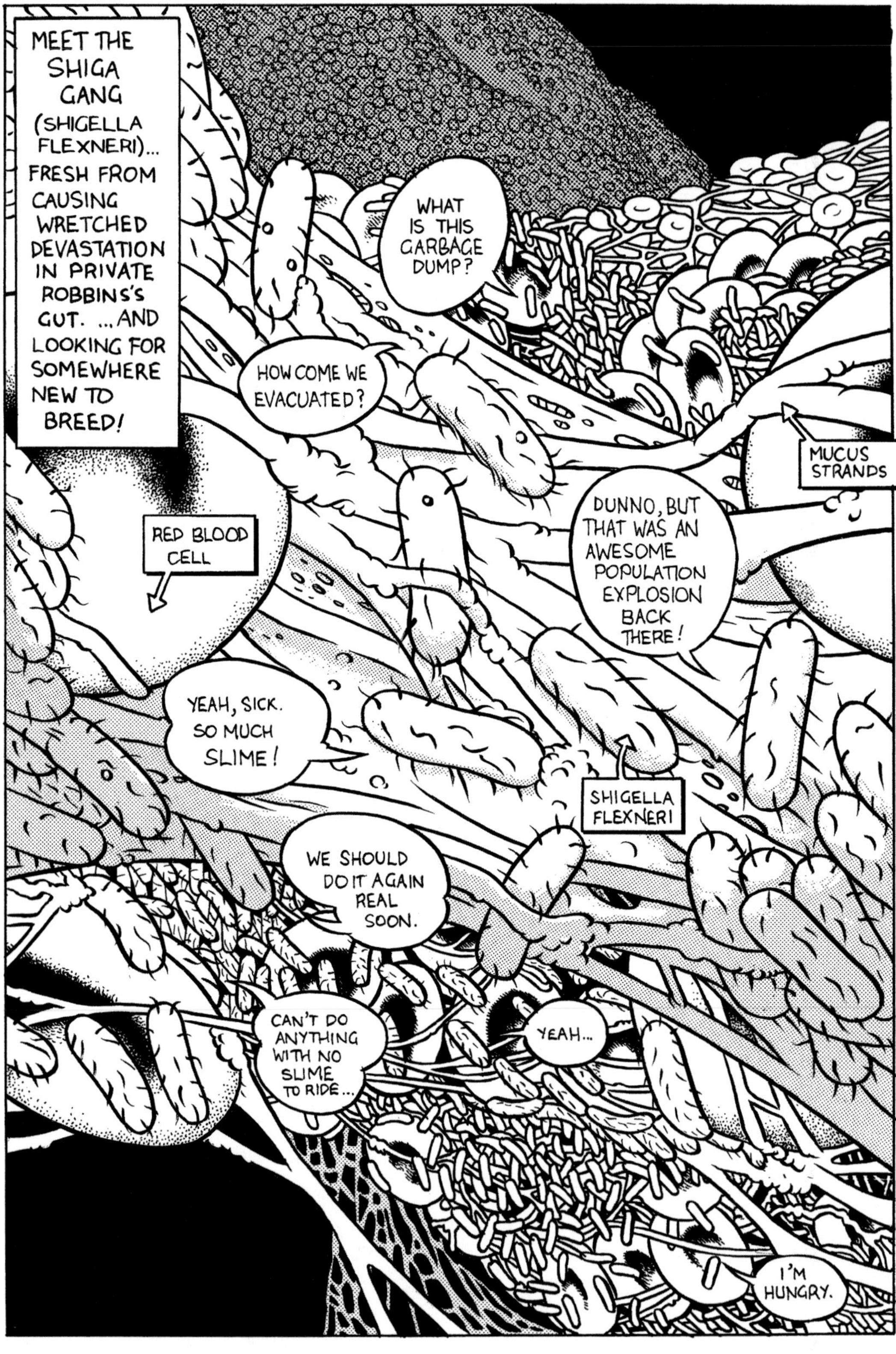
MEET THE SHIGA GANG (SHIGELLA FLEXNERI)... FRESH FROM CAUSING WRETCHED DEVASTATION IN PRIVATE ROBBINS'S GUT. ...AND LOOKING FOR SOMEWHERE NEW TO BREED!
WHAT IS THIS GARBAGE DUMP?
HOW COME WE EVACUATED?
MUCUS STRANDS
DUNNO, BUT THAT WAS AN AWESOME POPULATION EXPLOSION BACK THERE!
RED BLOOD CELL
YEAH, SICK. SO MUCH SLIME!
SHIGELLA FLEXNERI
WE SHOULD DO IT AGAIN REAL SOON.
CAN'T DO ANYTHING WITH NO SLIME TO RIDE...
YEAH...
I'M HUNGRY.

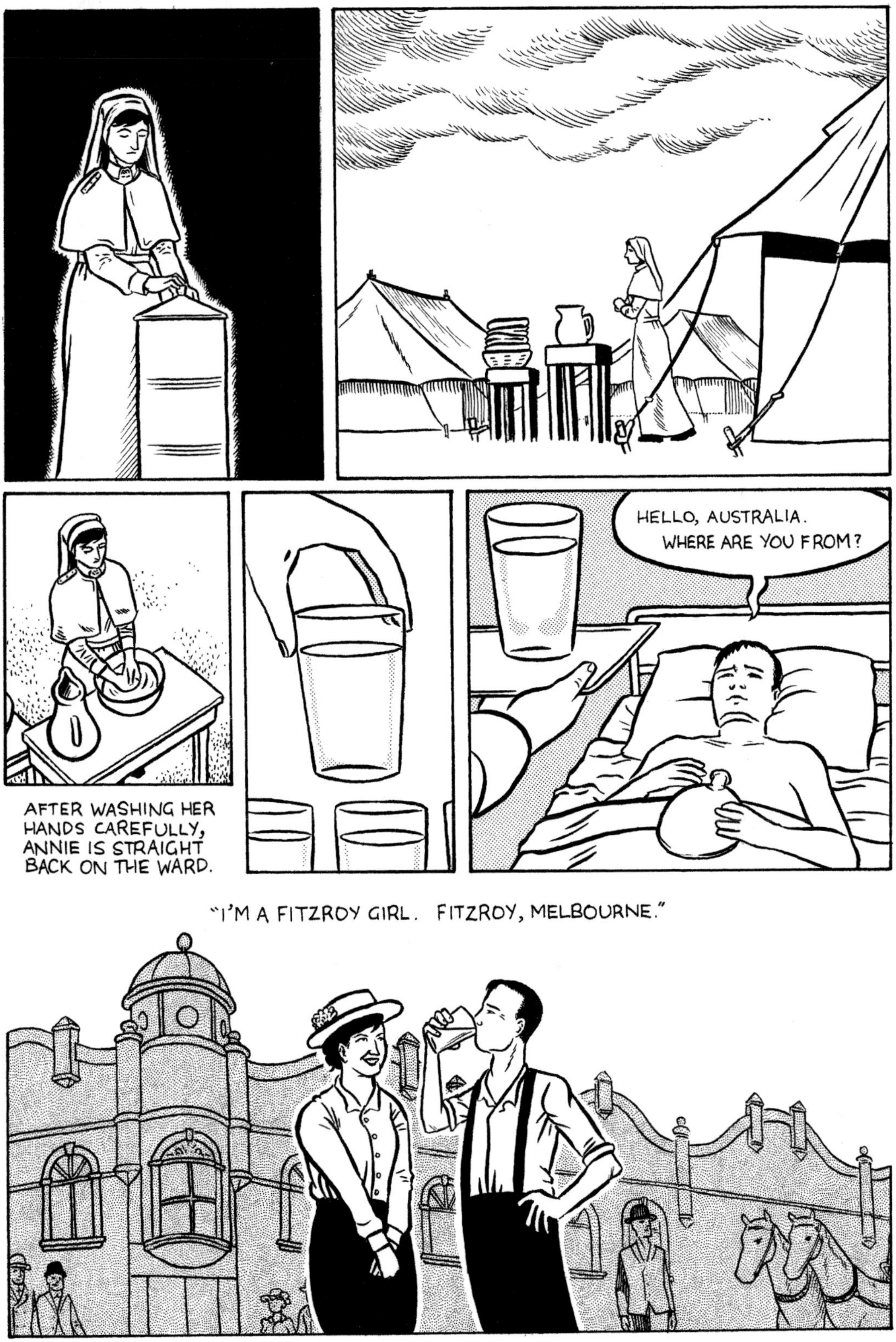
AFTER WASHING HER HANDS CAREFULLY, ANNIE IS STRAIGHT BACK ON THE WARD.
HELLO, AUSTRALIA. WHERE ARE YOU FROM?
"I'M A FITZROY GIRL. FITZROY, MELBOURNE."

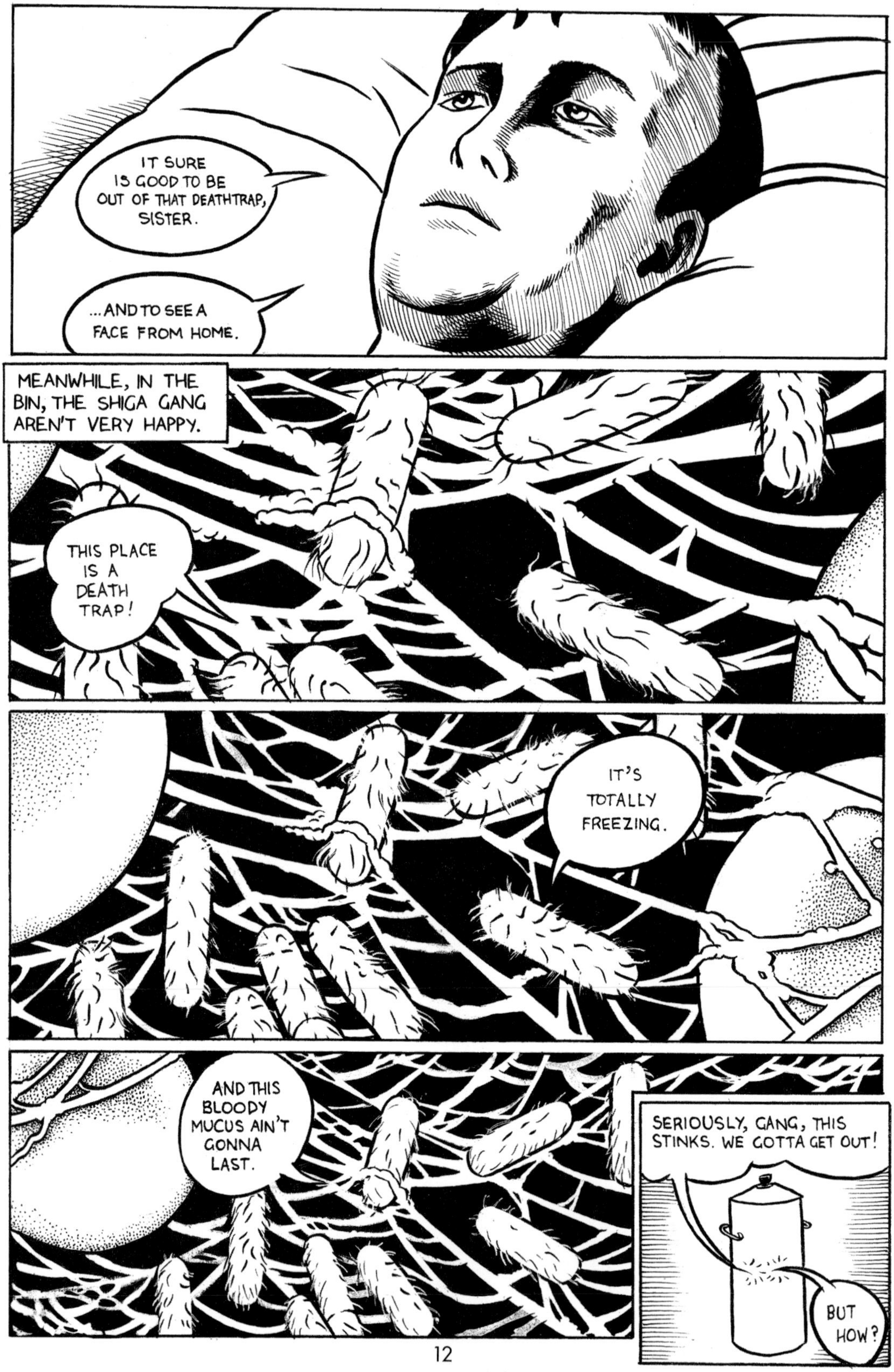
IT SURE IS GOOD TO BE OUT OF THAT DEATHTRAP, SISTER.
...AND TO SEE A FACE FROM HOME.
MEANWHILE, IN THE BIN, THE SHIGA GANG AREN'T VERY HAPPY.
THIS PLACE IS A DEATH TRAP!
IT'S TOTALLY FREEZING.
AND THIS BLOODY MUCUS AIN'T GONNA LAST.
SERIOUSLY, GANG, THIS STINKS. WE GOTTA GET OUT!
BUT HOW?

...WHILE THE REST OF THE SHIGA GANG, STILL INSIDE PRIVATE ROBBINS, ARE MAKING HIM MORE AND MORE WRETCHED.

SISTER, I GOTTA GO ALREADY.

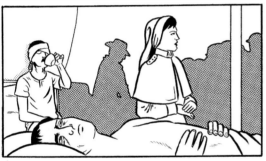

COMING, ROBBINS!

GOOD. I CAN TAKE A PURE STOOL SAMPLE - WITHOUT ANY TRENCH FILTH MIXED UP IN IT.

WASTE OF TIME.

SIR?

PUTTING FLUIDS UNDER MICROSCOPES IS NO SUBSTITUTE FOR PROPER MEDICINE!

DR. MACLEAN TOLD ME TO, SIR.

HE WOULD.

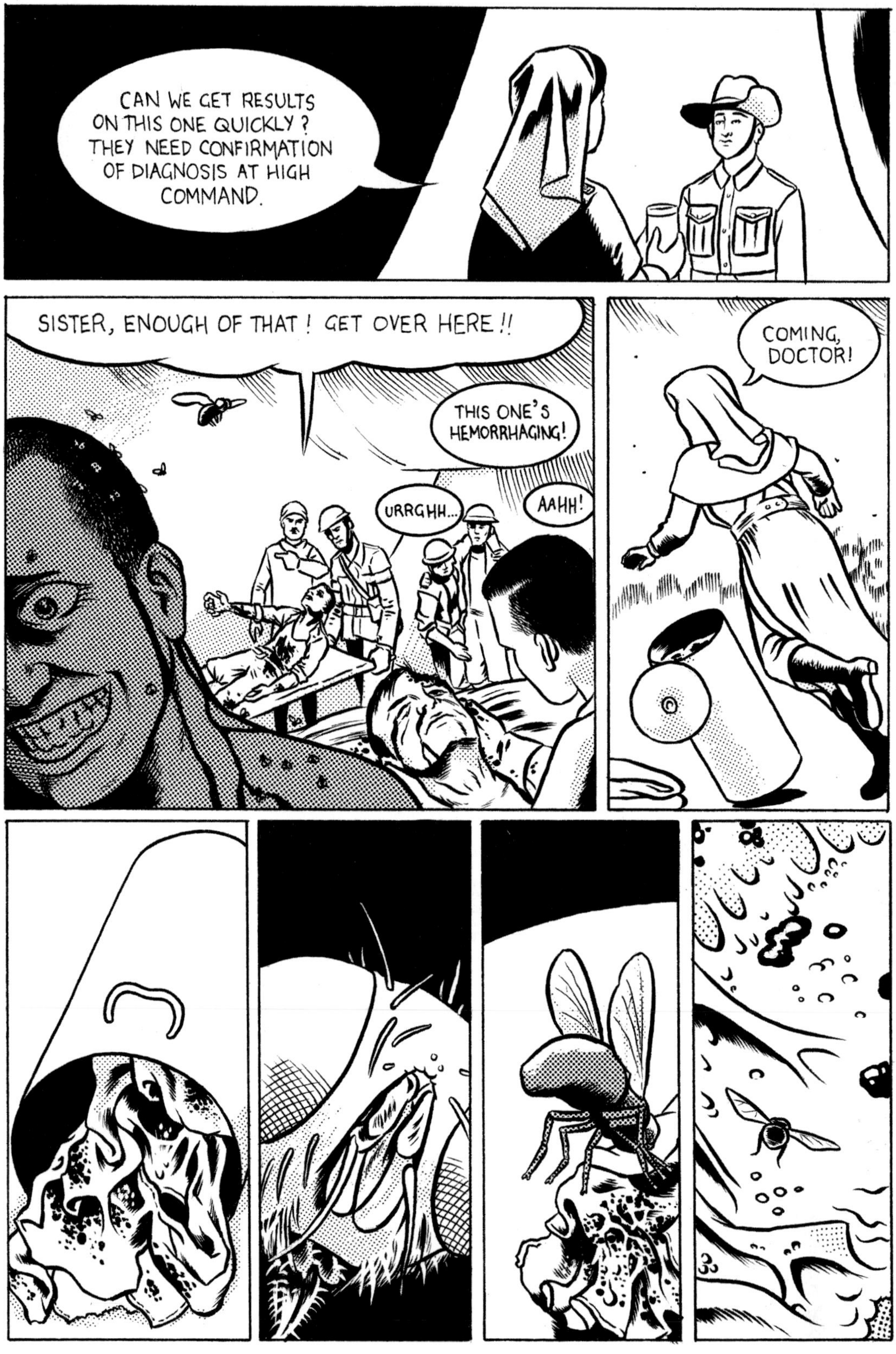
CAN WE GET RESULTS ON THIS ONE QUICKLY? THEY NEED CONFIRMATION OF DIAGNOSIS AT HIGH COMMAND.
SISTER, ENOUGH OF THAT! GET OVER HERE!!
THIS ONE'S HEMORRHAGING!
URRGHH...
AAHH!
COMING, DOCTOR!

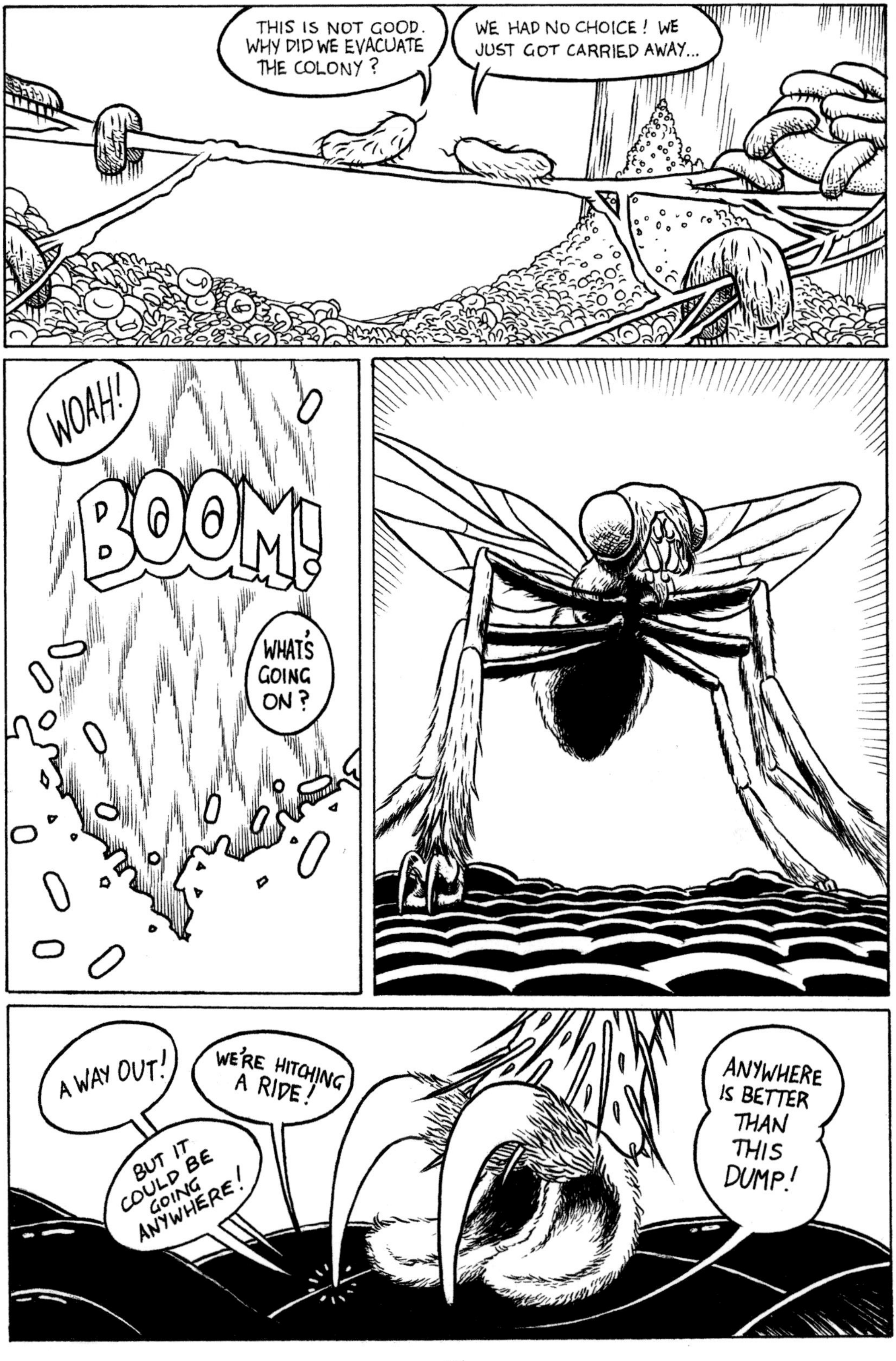
THIS IS NOT GOOD. WHY DID WE EVACUATE THE COLONY?
WE HAD NO CHOICE! WE JUST GOT CARRIED AWAY...
WOAH!
BOOM!
WHAT'S GOING ON?
A WAY OUT!
WE'RE HITCHING A RIDE!
BUT IT COULD BE GOING ANYWHERE!
ANYWHERE IS BETTER THAN THIS DUMP!

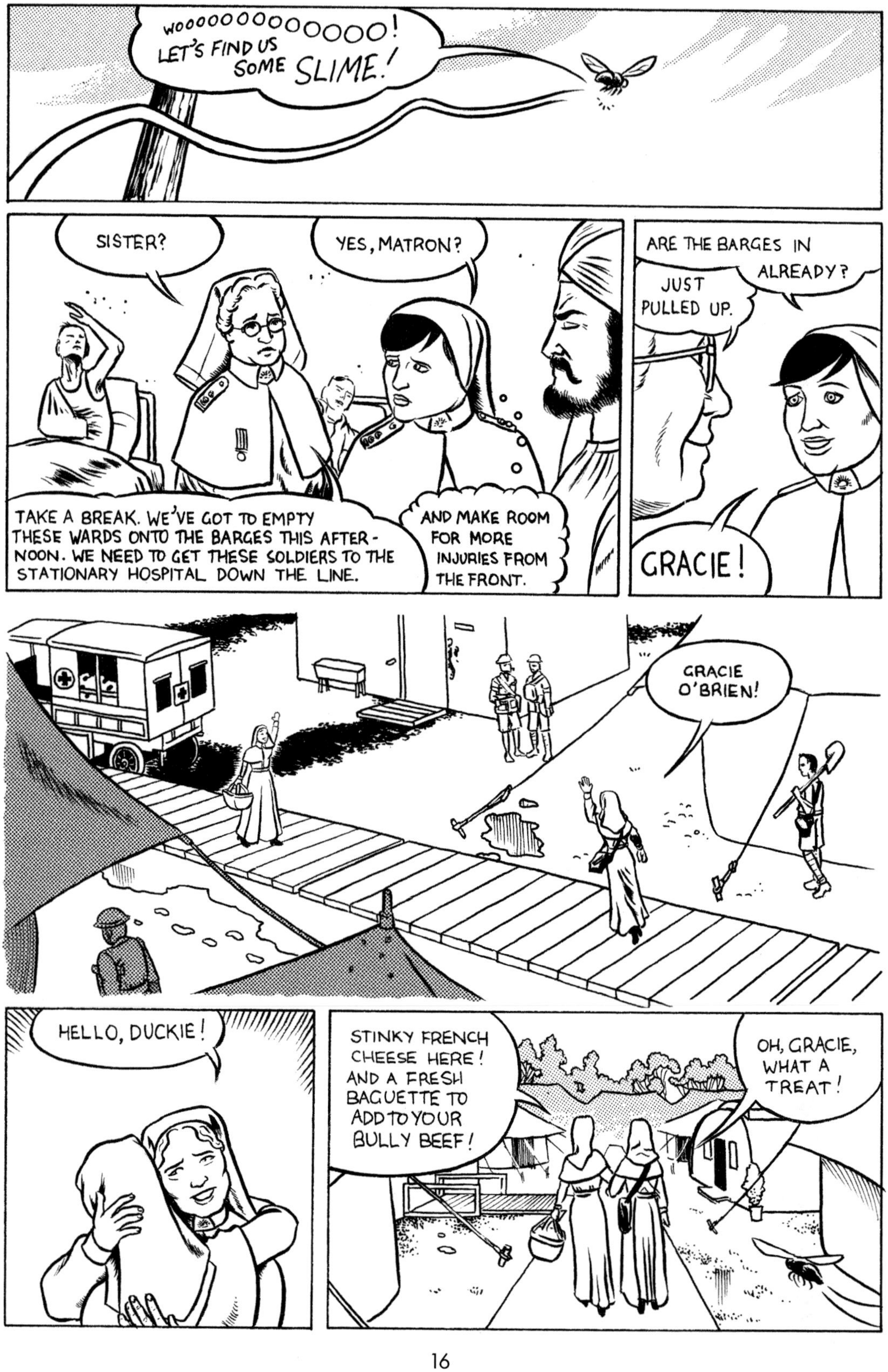
WOOOOOOOOOOOOOO! LET'S FIND US SOME SLIME!
SISTER?
YES, MATRON?
TAKE A BREAK. WE'VE GOT TO EMPTY THESE WARDS ONTO THE BARGES THIS AFTER-NOON. WE NEED TO GET THESE SOLDIERS TO THE STATIONARY HOSPITAL DOWN THE LINE.
AND MAKE ROOM FOR MORE INJURIES FROM THE FRONT.
ARE THE BARGES IN ALREADY?
JUST PULLED UP.
GRACIE!
GRACIE O'BRIEN!
HELLO, DUCKIE!
STINKY FRENCH CHEESE HERE! AND A FRESH BAGUETTE TO ADD TO YOUR BULLY BEEF!
OH, GRACIE, WHAT A TREAT!

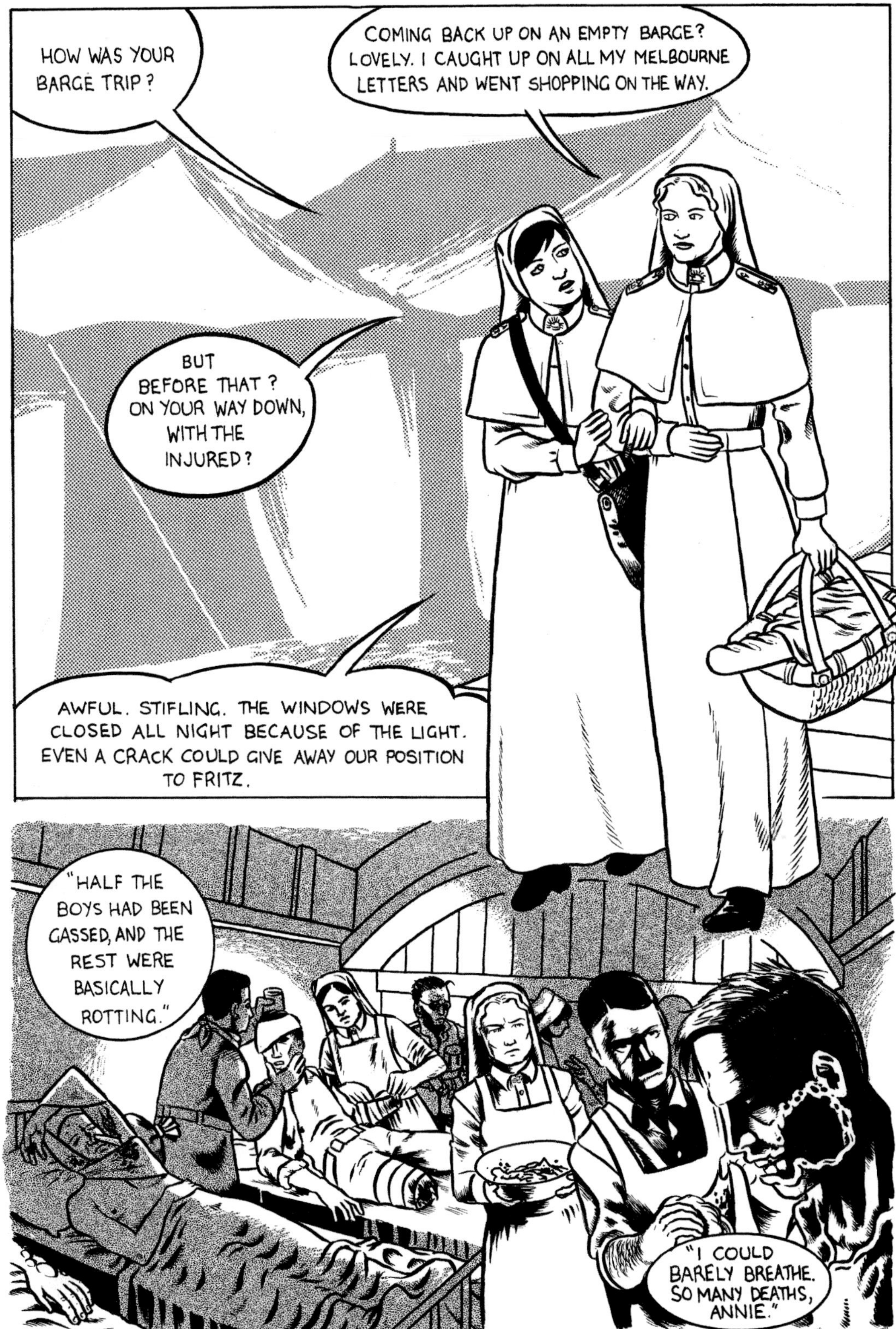
HOW WAS YOUR BARGE TRIP?
COMING BACK UP ON AN EMPTY BARGE? LOVELY. I CAUGHT UP ON ALL MY MELBOURNE LETTERS AND WENT SHOPPING ON THE WAY.
BUT BEFORE THAT? ON YOUR WAY DOWN, WITH THE INJURED?
AWFUL. STIFLING. THE WINDOWS WERE CLOSED ALL NIGHT BECAUSE OF THE LIGHT. EVEN A CRACK COULD GIVE AWAY OUR POSITION TO FRITZ.
"HALF THE BOYS HAD BEEN GASSED, AND THE REST WERE BASICALLY ROTTING."
"I COULD BARELY BREATHE. SO MANY DEATHS, ANNIE."

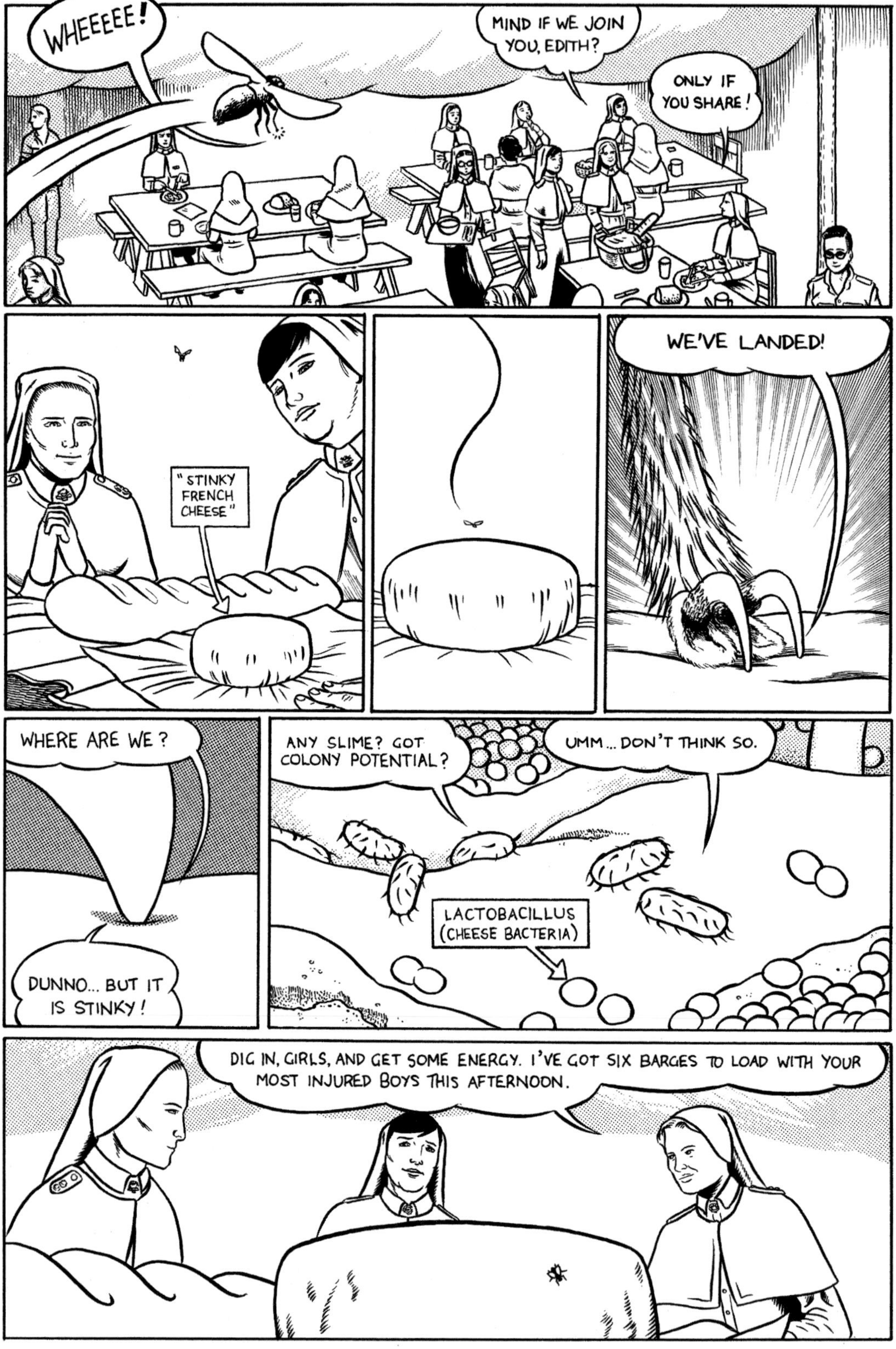

WHEEEEE!
MIND IF WE JOIN YOU, EDITH?
ONLY IF YOU SHARE!
"STINKY FRENCH CHEESE"
WE'VE LANDED!
WHERE ARE WE?
DUNNO... BUT IT IS STINKY!
ANY SLIME? GOT COLONY POTENTIAL?
UMM... DON'T THINK SO.
LACTOBACILLUS (CHEESE BACTERIA)
DIG IN, GIRLS, AND GET SOME ENERGY. I'VE GOT SIX BARGES TO LOAD WITH YOUR MOST INJURED BOYS THIS AFTERNOON.

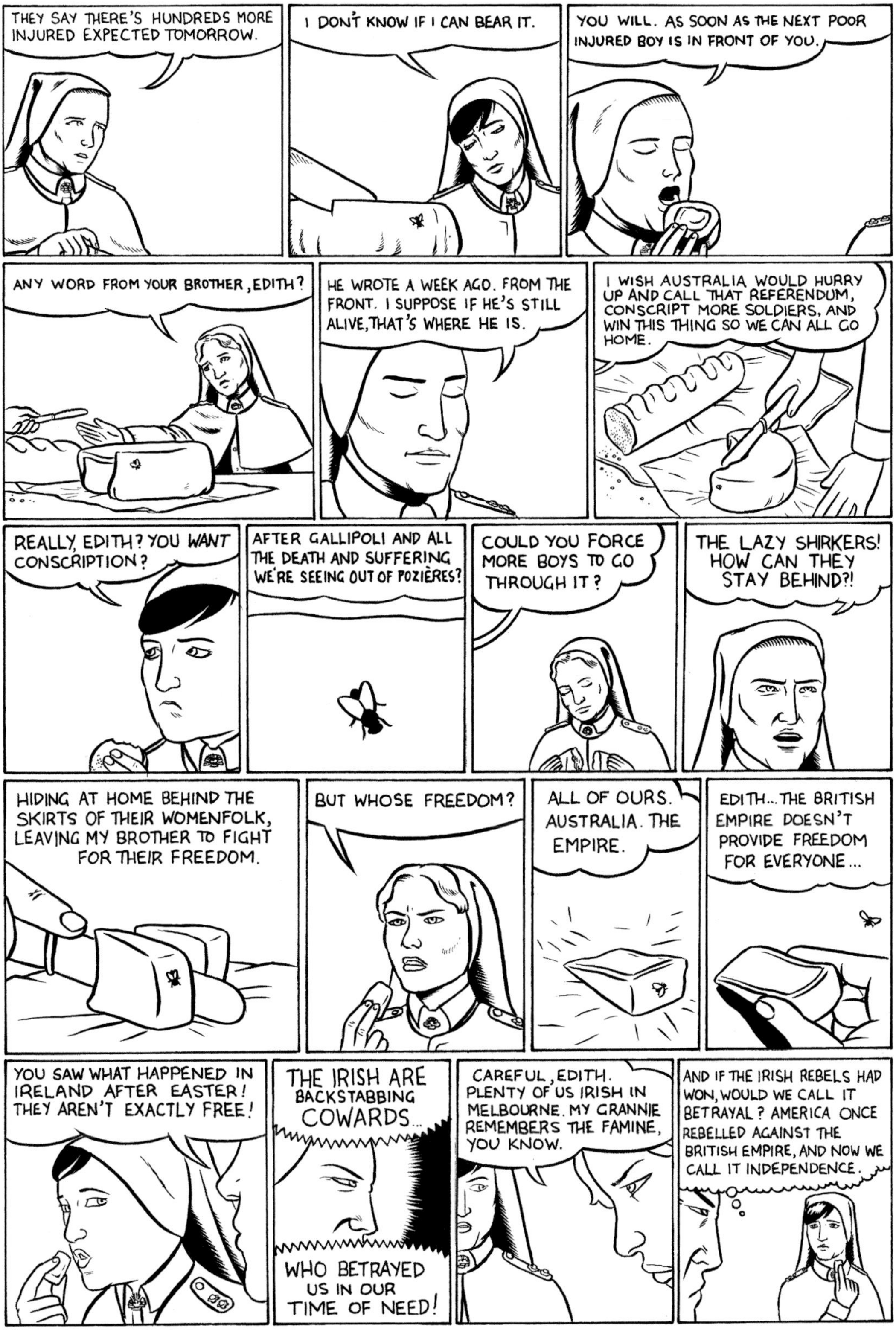
THEY SAY THERE'S HUNDREDS MORE INJURED EXPECTED TOMORROW.
I DON'T KNOW IF I CAN BEAR IT.
YOU WILL. AS SOON AS THE NEXT POOR INJURED BOY IS IN FRONT OF YOU.
ANY WORD FROM YOUR BROTHER, EDITH?
HE WROTE A WEEK AGO. FROM THE FRONT. I SUPPOSE IF HE'S STILL ALIVE, THAT'S WHERE HE IS.
I WISH AUSTRALIA WOULD HURRY UP AND CALL THAT REFERENDUM, CONSCRIPT MORE SOLDIERS, AND WIN THIS THING SO WE CAN ALL GO HOME.
REALLY, EDITH? YOU *WANT* CONSCRIPTION?
AFTER GALLIPOLI AND ALL THE DEATH AND SUFFERING WE'RE SEEING OUT OF POZIÈRES?
COULD YOU FORCE MORE BOYS TO GO THROUGH IT?
THE LAZY SHIRKERS! HOW CAN THEY STAY BEHIND?!
HIDING AT HOME BEHIND THE SKIRTS OF THEIR WOMENFOLK, LEAVING MY BROTHER TO FIGHT FOR THEIR FREEDOM.
BUT WHOSE FREEDOM?
ALL OF OURS. AUSTRALIA. THE EMPIRE.
EDITH... THE BRITISH EMPIRE DOESN'T PROVIDE FREEDOM FOR EVERYONE...
YOU SAW WHAT HAPPENED IN IRELAND AFTER EASTER! THEY AREN'T EXACTLY FREE!
THE IRISH ARE BACKSTABBING COWARDS...
WHO BETRAYED US IN OUR TIME OF NEED!
CAREFUL, EDITH. PLENTY OF US IRISH IN MELBOURNE. MY GRANNIE REMEMBERS THE FAMINE, YOU KNOW.
AND IF THE IRISH REBELS HAD WON, WOULD WE CALL IT BETRAYAL? AMERICA ONCE REBELLED AGAINST THE BRITISH EMPIRE, AND NOW WE CALL IT INDEPENDENCE.

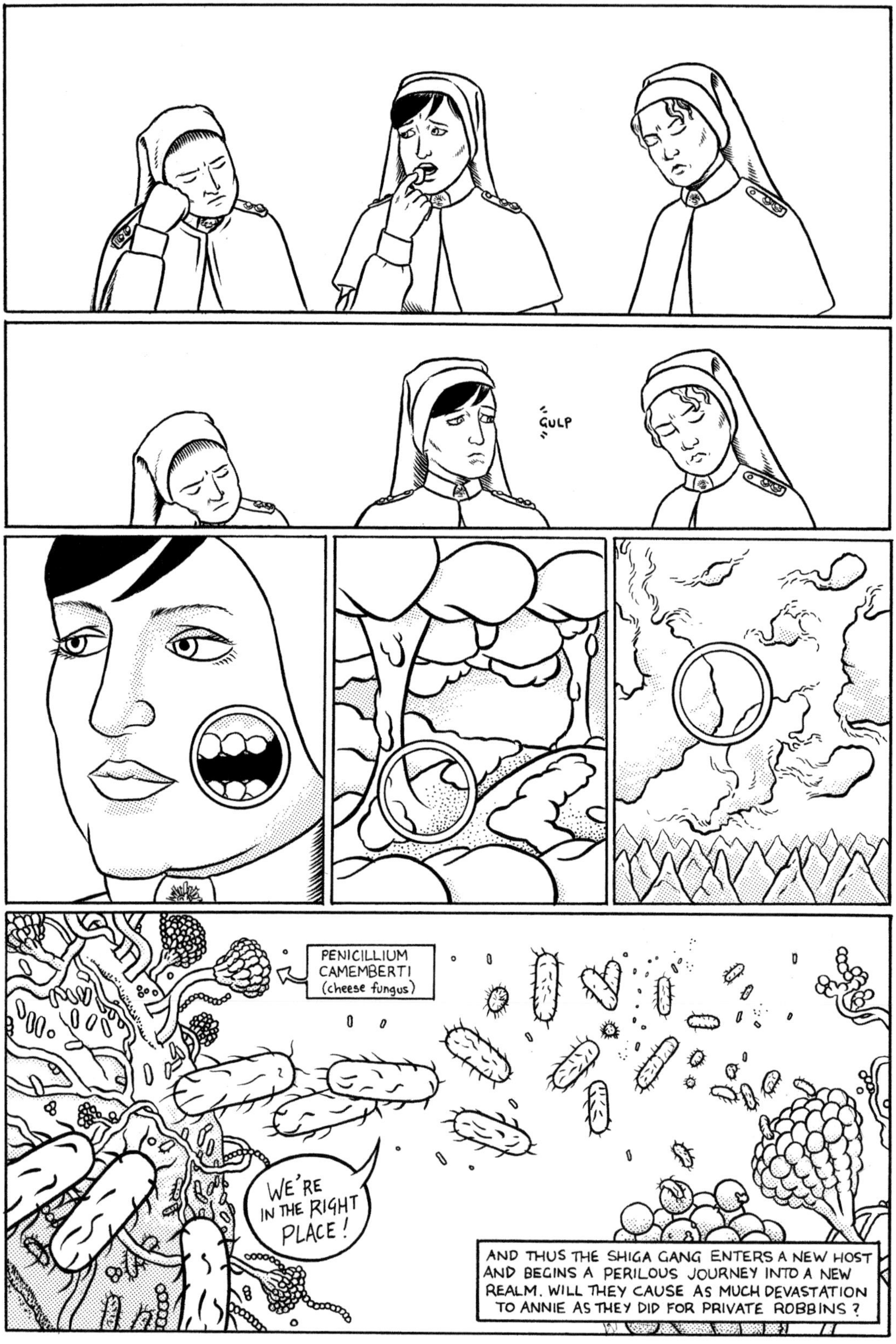
GULP
PENICILLIUM CAMEMBERTI (cheese fungus)
WE'RE IN THE RIGHT PLACE!
AND THUS THE SHIGA GANG ENTERS A NEW HOST AND BEGINS A PERILOUS JOURNEY INTO A NEW REALM. WILL THEY CAUSE AS MUCH DEVASTATION TO ANNIE AS THEY DID FOR PRIVATE ROBBINS?

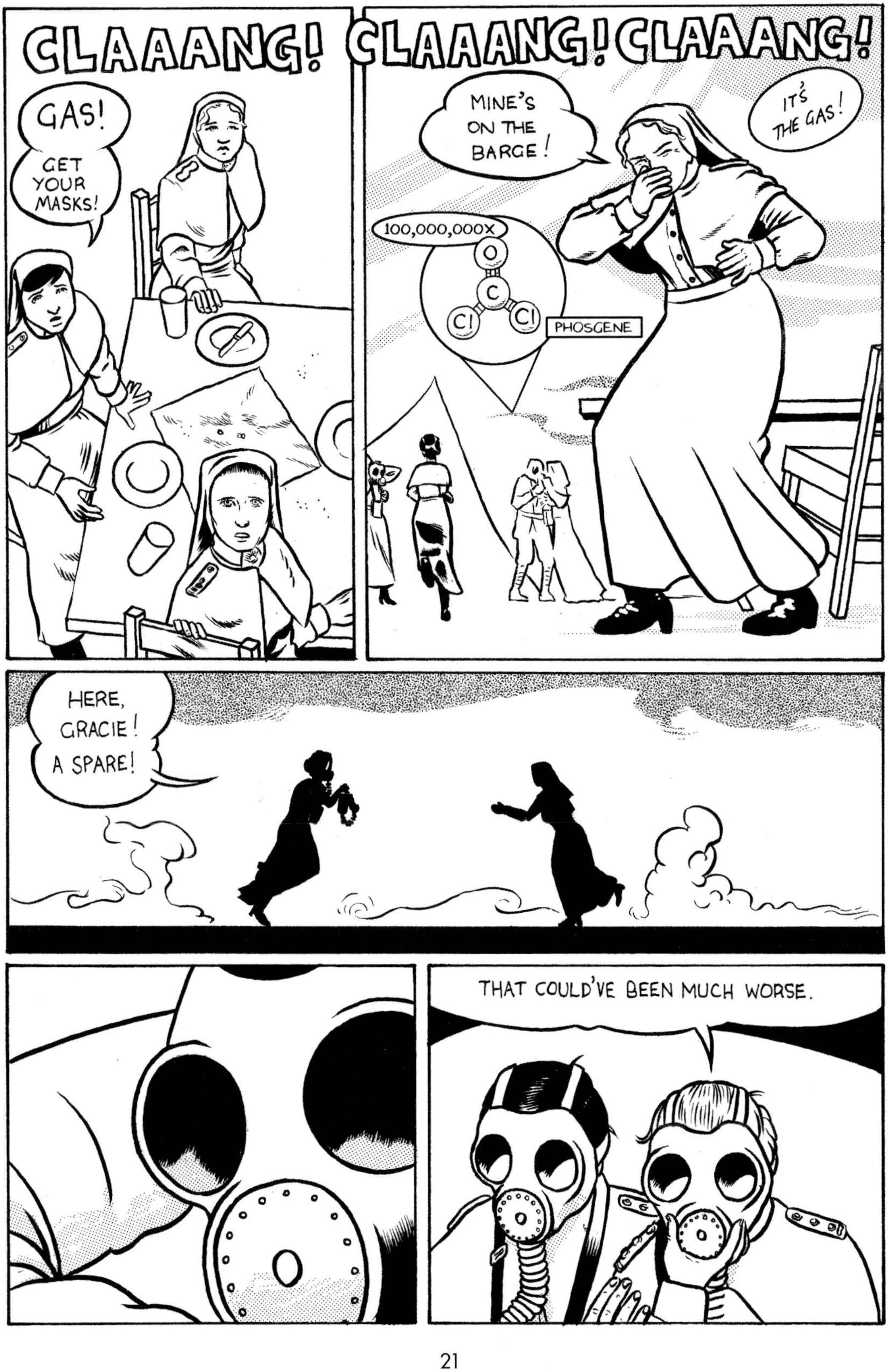
CLAAANG! CLAAANG! CLAAANG!
GAS!
GET YOUR MASKS!
MINE'S ON THE BARGE!
IT'S THE GAS!
100,000,000X
O
C
Cl
Cl
PHOSGENE
HERE, GRACIE! A SPARE!
THAT COULD'VE BEEN MUCH WORSE.

AS ANNIE BREATHES ANXIOUSLY THROUGH HER GAS MASK, THE SHIGA GANG SLIDE DOWN...

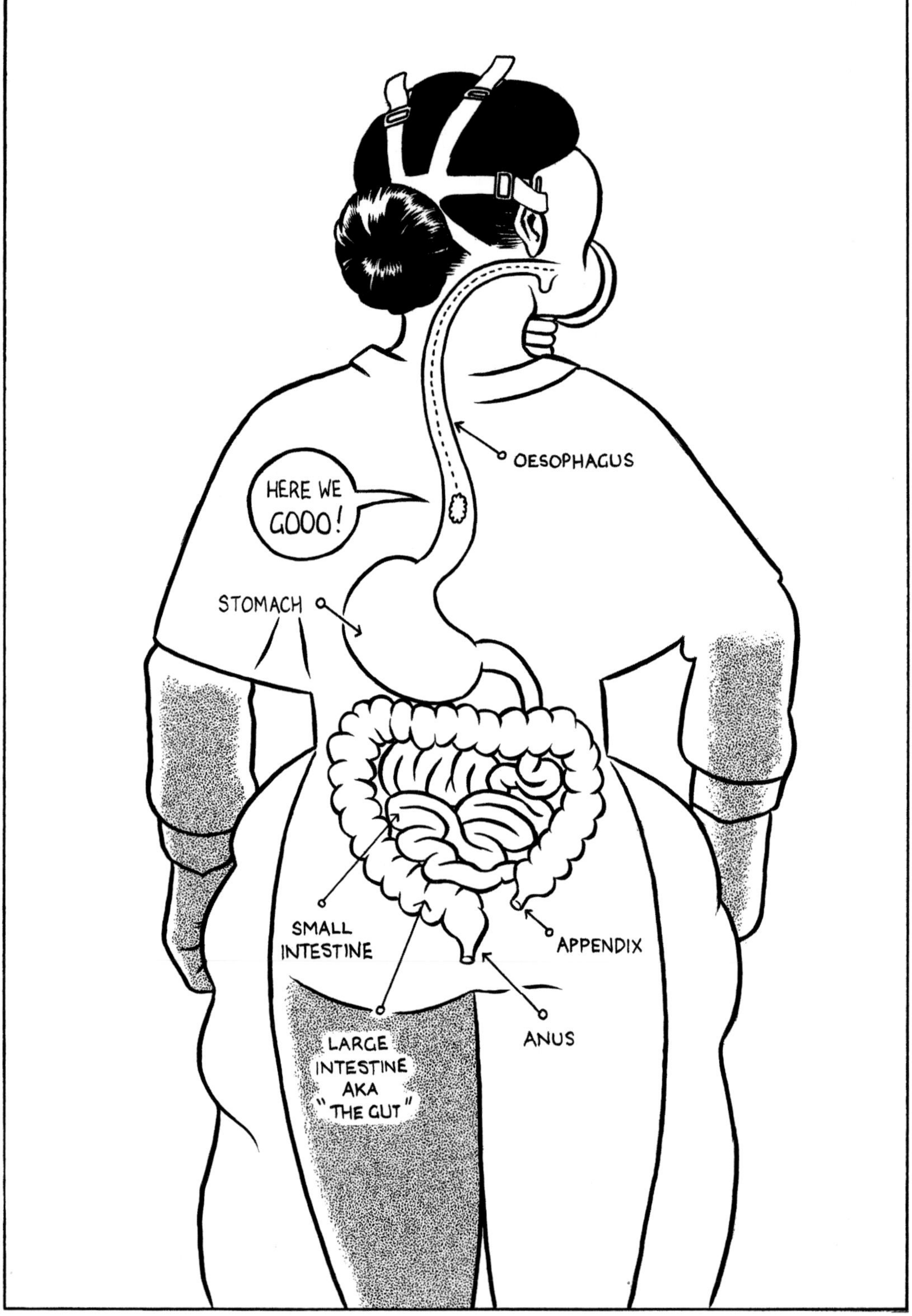
OESOPHAGUS
HERE WE GOOO!
STOMACH
SMALL INTESTINE
APPENDIX
ANUS
LARGE INTESTINE AKA "THE GUT"

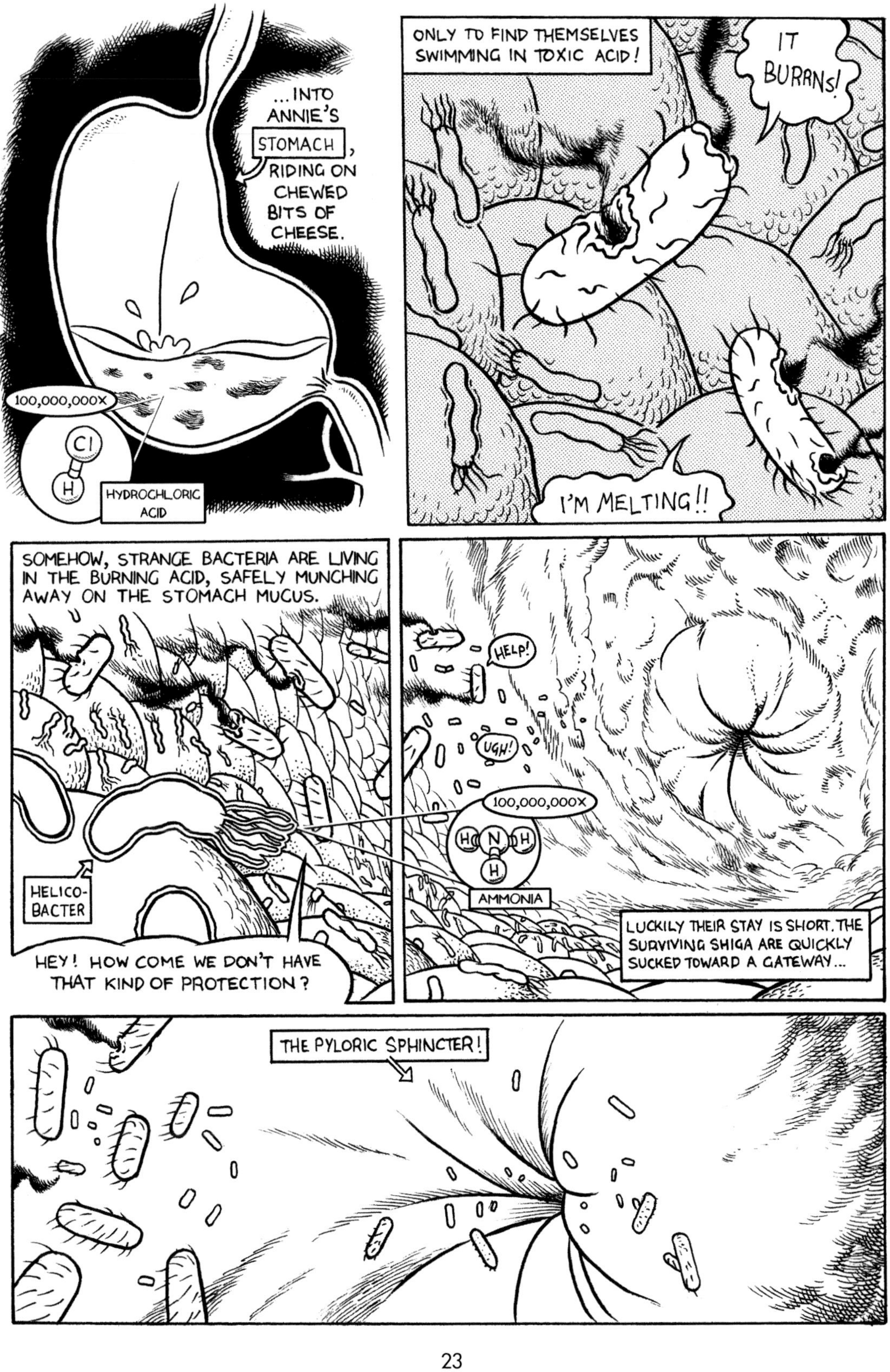
...INTO ANNIE'S STOMACH, RIDING ON CHEWED BITS OF CHEESE.
STOMACH
100,000,000X
Cl
H
HYDROCHLORIC ACID
ONLY TO FIND THEMSELVES SWIMMING IN TOXIC ACID!
IT BURRNS!
I'M MELTING!!
SOMEHOW, STRANGE BACTERIA ARE LIVING IN THE BURNING ACID, SAFELY MUNCHING AWAY ON THE STOMACH MUCUS.
HELICO-BACTER
HEY! HOW COME WE DON'T HAVE THAT KIND OF PROTECTION?
HELP!
UGH!
100,000,000X
H N H
H
AMMONIA
LUCKILY THEIR STAY IS SHORT. THE SURVIVING SHIGA ARE QUICKLY SUCKED TOWARD A GATEWAY...
THE PYLORIC SPHINCTER!

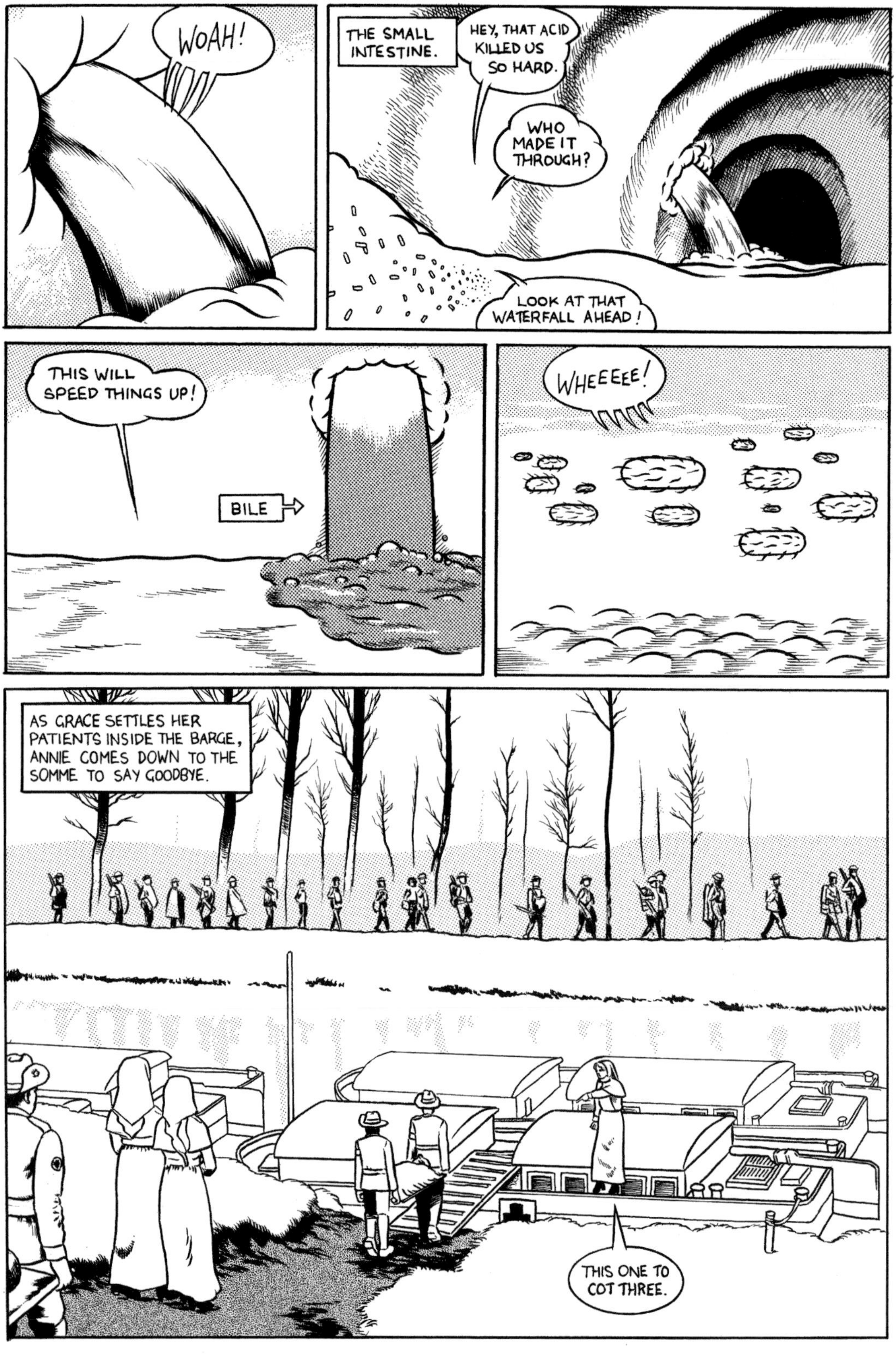
WOAH!
THE SMALL INTESTINE.
HEY, THAT ACID KILLED US SO HARD.
WHO MADE IT THROUGH?
LOOK AT THAT WATERFALL AHEAD!
THIS WILL SPEED THINGS UP!
BILE
WHEEEEE!
AS GRACE SETTLES HER PATIENTS INSIDE THE BARGE, ANNIE COMES DOWN TO THE SOMME TO SAY GOODBYE.
THIS ONE TO COT THREE.

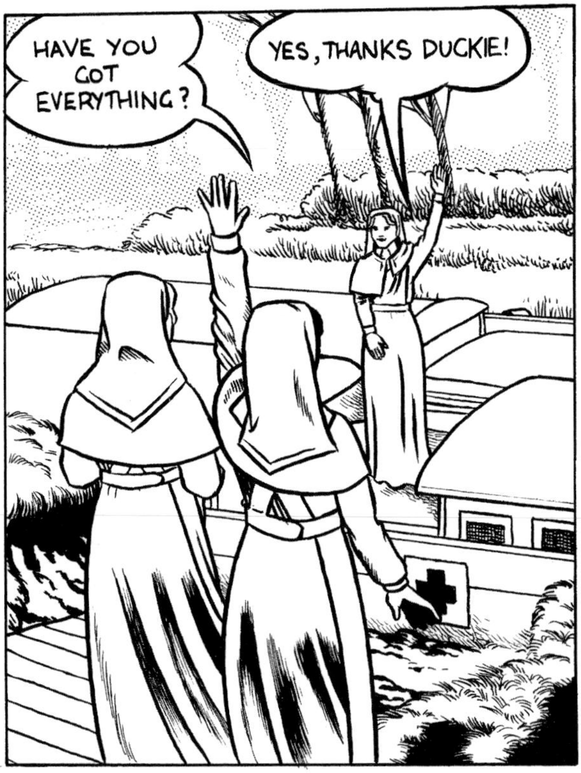
HAVE YOU GOT EVERYTHING?
YES, THANKS DUCKIE!

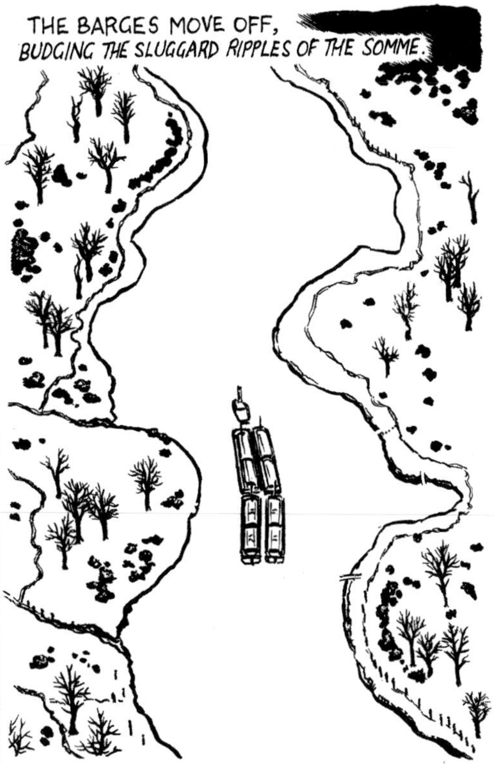
THE BARGES MOVE OFF, BUDGING THE SLUGGARD RIPPLES OF THE SOMME.

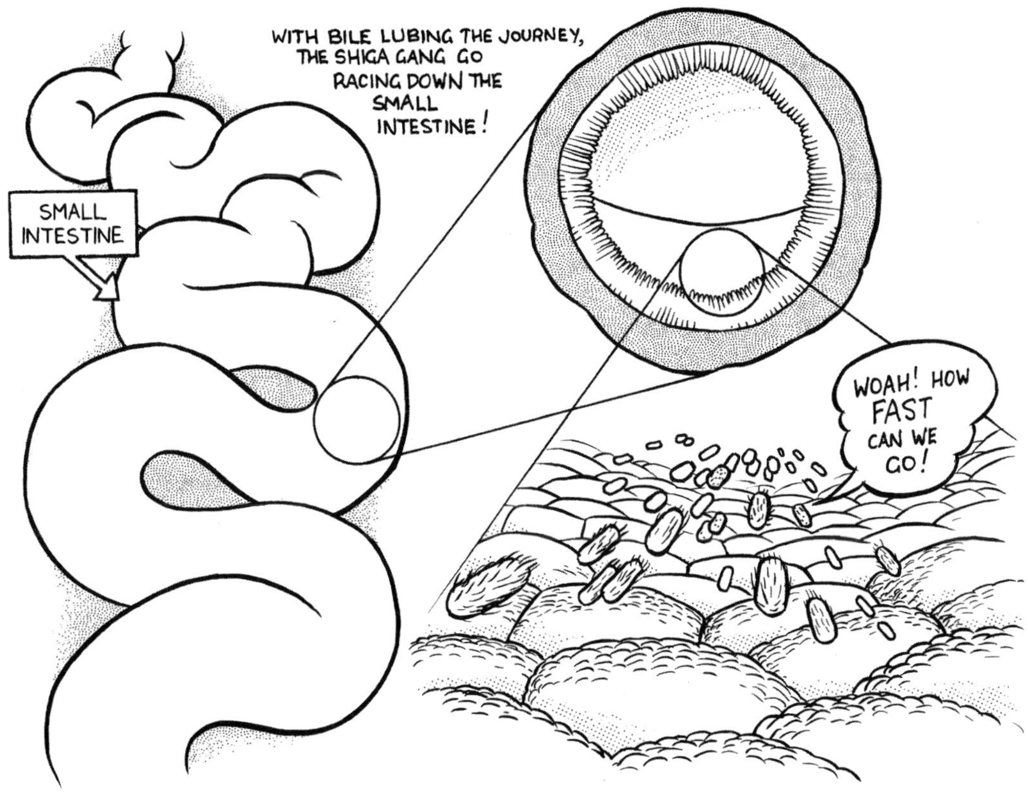
WITH BILE LUBING THE JOURNEY, THE SHIGA GANG GO RACING DOWN THE SMALL INTESTINE!
SMALL INTESTINE
WOAH! HOW FAST CAN WE GO!

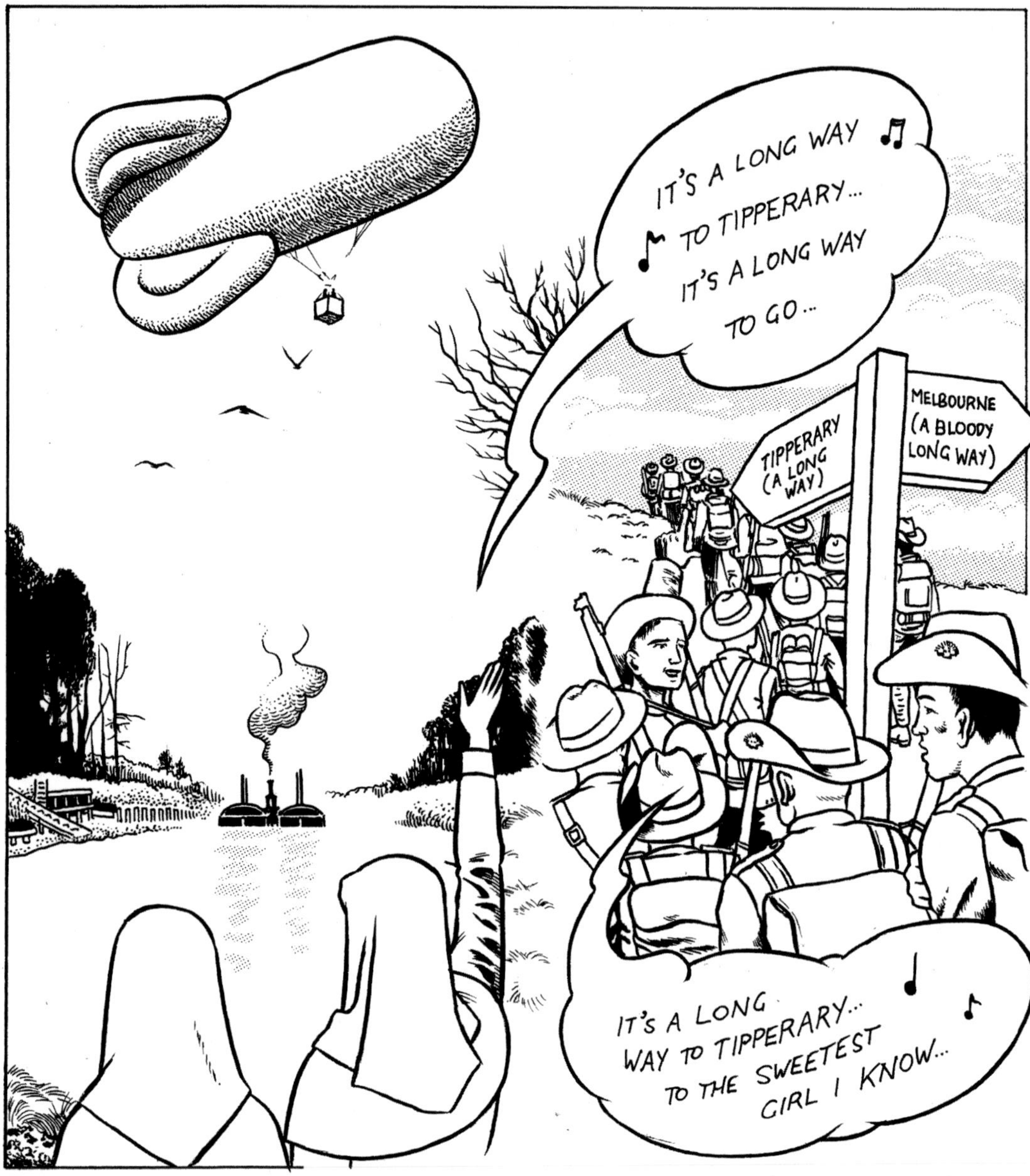
IT'S A LONG WAY TO TIPPERARY... IT'S A LONG WAY IT'S A LONG WAY TO GO...
MELBOURNE (A BLOODY LONG WAY)
TIPPERARY (A LONG WAY)
IT'S A LONG WAY TO TIPPERARY... TO THE SWEETEST GIRL I KNOW...

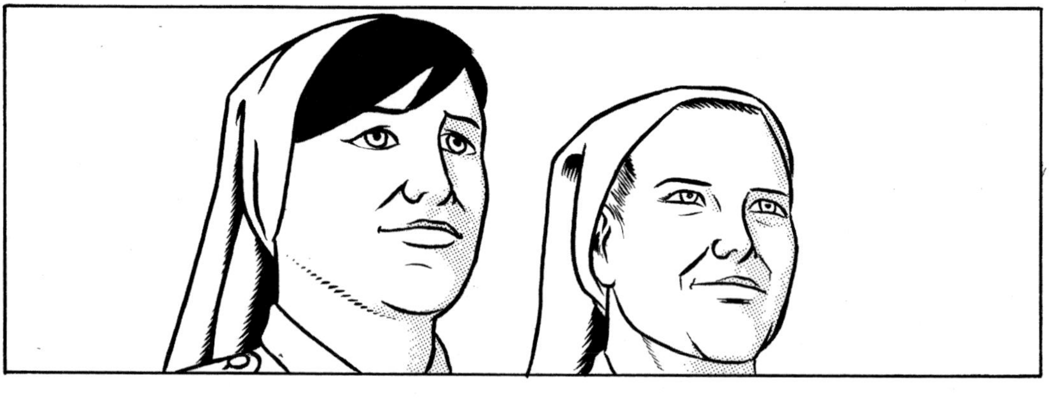

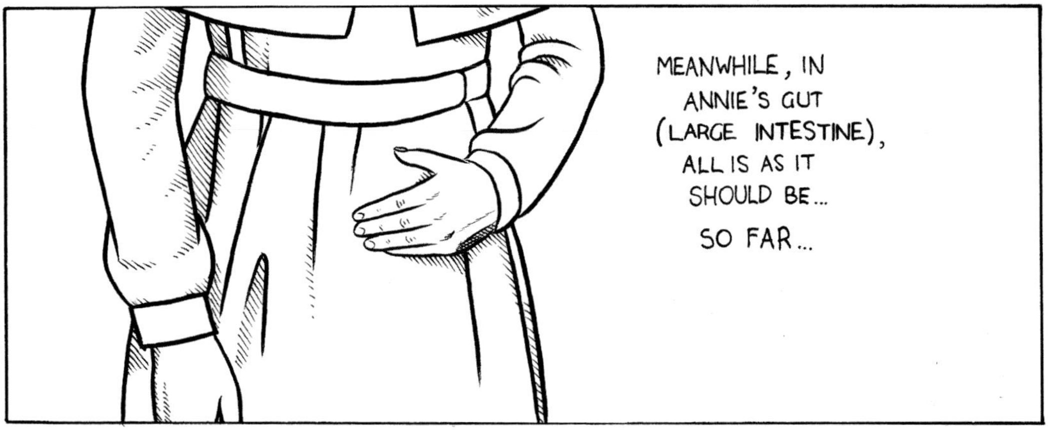
MEANWHILE, IN ANNIE'S GUT (LARGE INTESTINE), ALL IS AS IT SHOULD BE...
SO FAR...

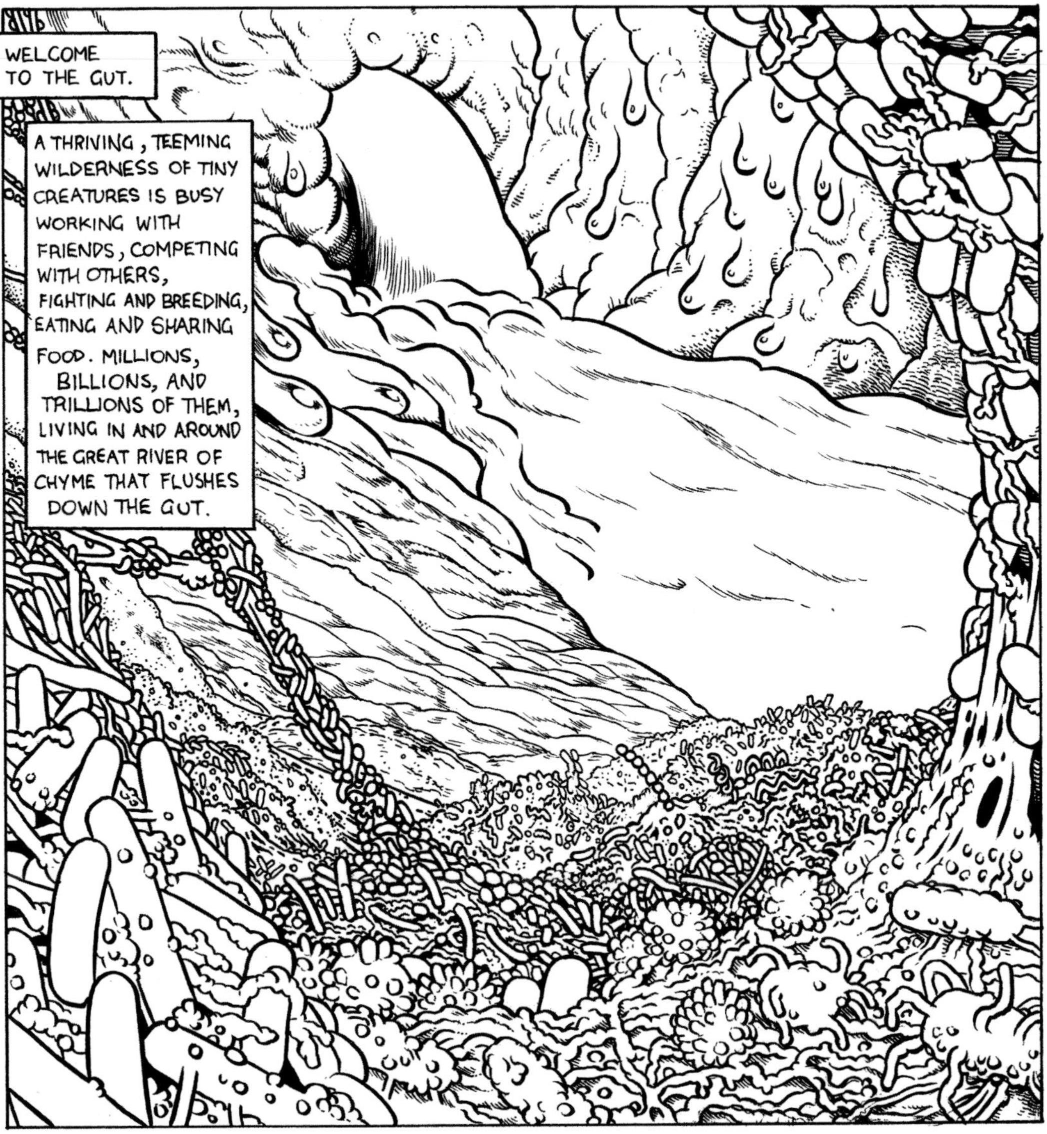
WELCOME TO THE GUT.
A THRIVING, TEEMING WILDERNESS OF TINY CREATURES IS BUSY WORKING WITH FRIENDS, COMPETING WITH OTHERS, FIGHTING AND BREEDING, EATING AND SHARING FOOD. MILLIONS, BILLIONS, AND TRILLIONS OF THEM, LIVING IN AND AROUND THE GREAT RIVER OF CHYME THAT FLUSHES DOWN THE GUT.

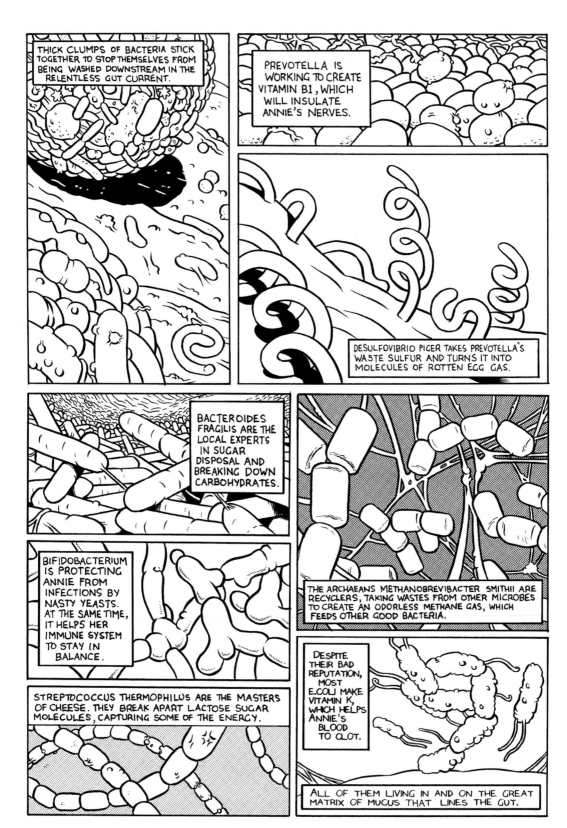

THICK CLUMPS OF BACTERIA STICK TOGETHER TO STOP THEMSELVES FROM BEING WASHED DOWNSTREAM IN THE RELENTLESS GUT CURRENT.

PREVOTELLA IS WORKING TO CREATE VITAMIN B1, WHICH WILL INSULATE ANNIE'S NERVES.

DESULFOVIBRIO PIGER TAKES PREVOTELLA'S WASTE SULFUR AND TURNS IT INTO MOLECULES OF ROTTEN EGG GAS.

BACTEROIDES FRAGILIS ARE THE LOCAL EXPERTS IN SUGAR DISPOSAL AND BREAKING DOWN CARBOHYDRATES.

THE ARCHAEANS METHANOBREVIBACTER SMITHII ARE RECYCLERS, TAKING WASTES FROM OTHER MICROBES TO CREATE AN ODORLESS METHANE GAS, WHICH FEEDS OTHER GOOD BACTERIA.

BIFIDOBACTERIUM IS PROTECTING ANNIE FROM INFECTIONS BY NASTY YEASTS. AT THE SAME TIME, IT HELPS HER IMMUNE SYSTEM TO STAY IN BALANCE.

DESPITE THEIR BAD REPUTATION, MOST E.COLI MAKE VITAMIN K, WHICH HELPS ANNIE'S BLOOD TO CLOT.

STREPTOCOCCUS THERMOPHILUS ARE THE MASTERS OF CHEESE. THEY BREAK APART LACTOSE SUGAR MOLECULES, CAPTURING SOME OF THE ENERGY.

ALL OF THEM LIVING IN AND ON THE GREAT MATRIX OF MUCUS THAT LINES THE GUT.

BUT EVEN DEEPER
WITHIN THE
MUCUS...

...DWELL THE PHAGE.
A VAST SWARM
OF VIRUSES.
TINY. EFFICIENT.
DEADLY.
(TO BACTERIA.)

WE HUNT AND CONNECT...

KILL AND PROTECT...

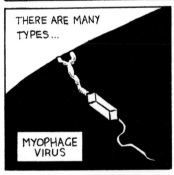

THERE ARE MANY
TYPES...

MYOPHAGE
VIRUS

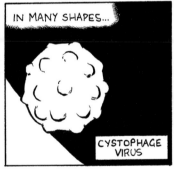

IN MANY SHAPES...

CYSTOPHAGE
VIRUS

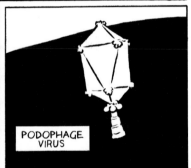

PODOPHAGE
VIRUS

SIPHOPHAGE
VIRUS

BUT THEY ALL DO A SIMILAR JOB.

PODOPHAGE
VIRUS

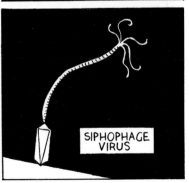

SIPHOPHAGE
VIRUS

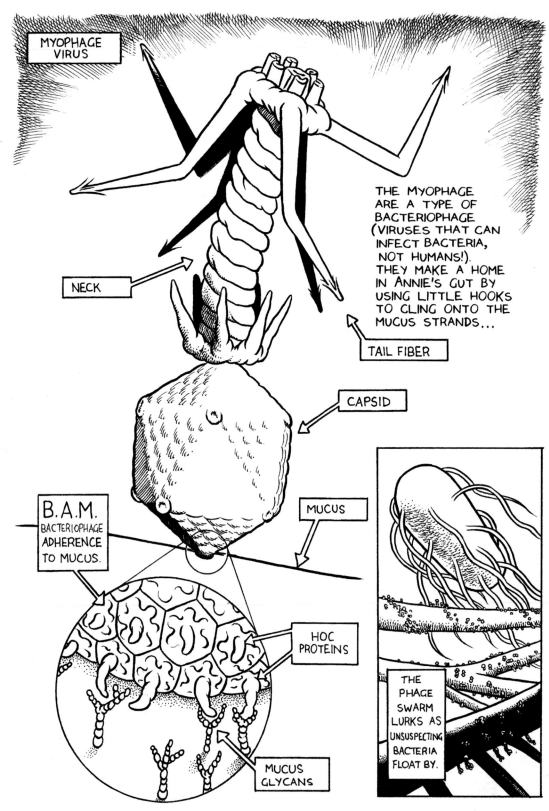

MYOPHAGE VIRUS

NECK

TAIL FIBER

CAPSID

THE MYOPHAGE ARE A TYPE OF BACTERIOPHAGE (VIRUSES THAT CAN INFECT BACTERIA, NOT HUMANS!). THEY MAKE A HOME IN ANNIE'S GUT BY USING LITTLE HOOKS TO CLING ONTO THE MUCUS STRANDS...

B.A.M. BACTERIOPHAGE ADHERENCE TO MUCUS.

MUCUS

HOC PROTEINS

MUCUS GLYCANS

THE PHAGE SWARM LURKS AS UNSUSPECTING BACTERIA FLOAT BY.

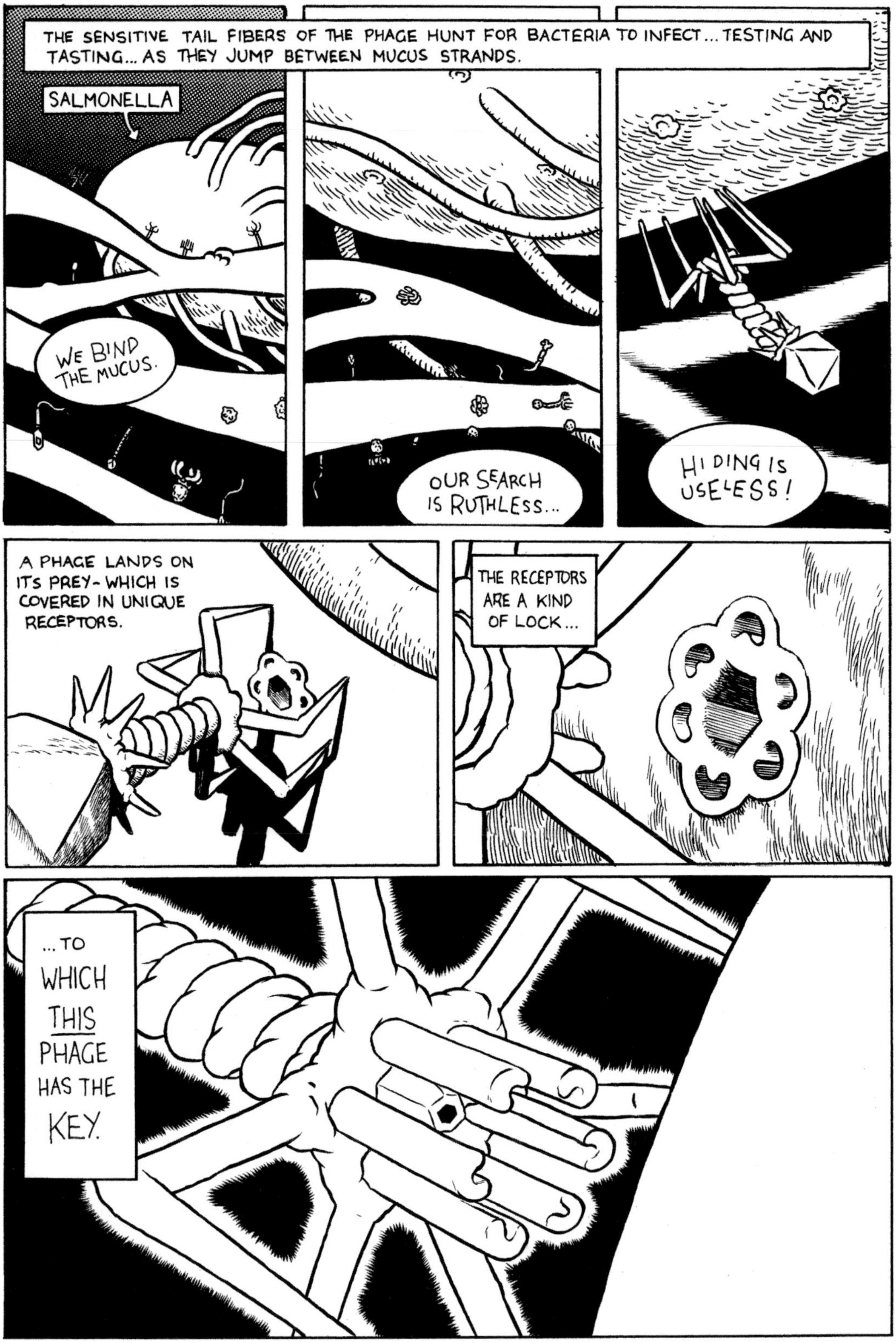

THE SENSITIVE TAIL FIBERS OF THE PHAGE HUNT FOR BACTERIA TO INFECT... TESTING AND TASTING... AS THEY JUMP BETWEEN MUCUS STRANDS.
SALMONELLA
WE BIND THE MUCUS.
OUR SEARCH IS RUTHLESS...
HIDING IS USELESS!
A PHAGE LANDS ON ITS PREY- WHICH IS COVERED IN UNIQUE RECEPTORS.
THE RECEPTORS ARE A KIND OF LOCK...
...TO WHICH THIS PHAGE HAS THE KEY.

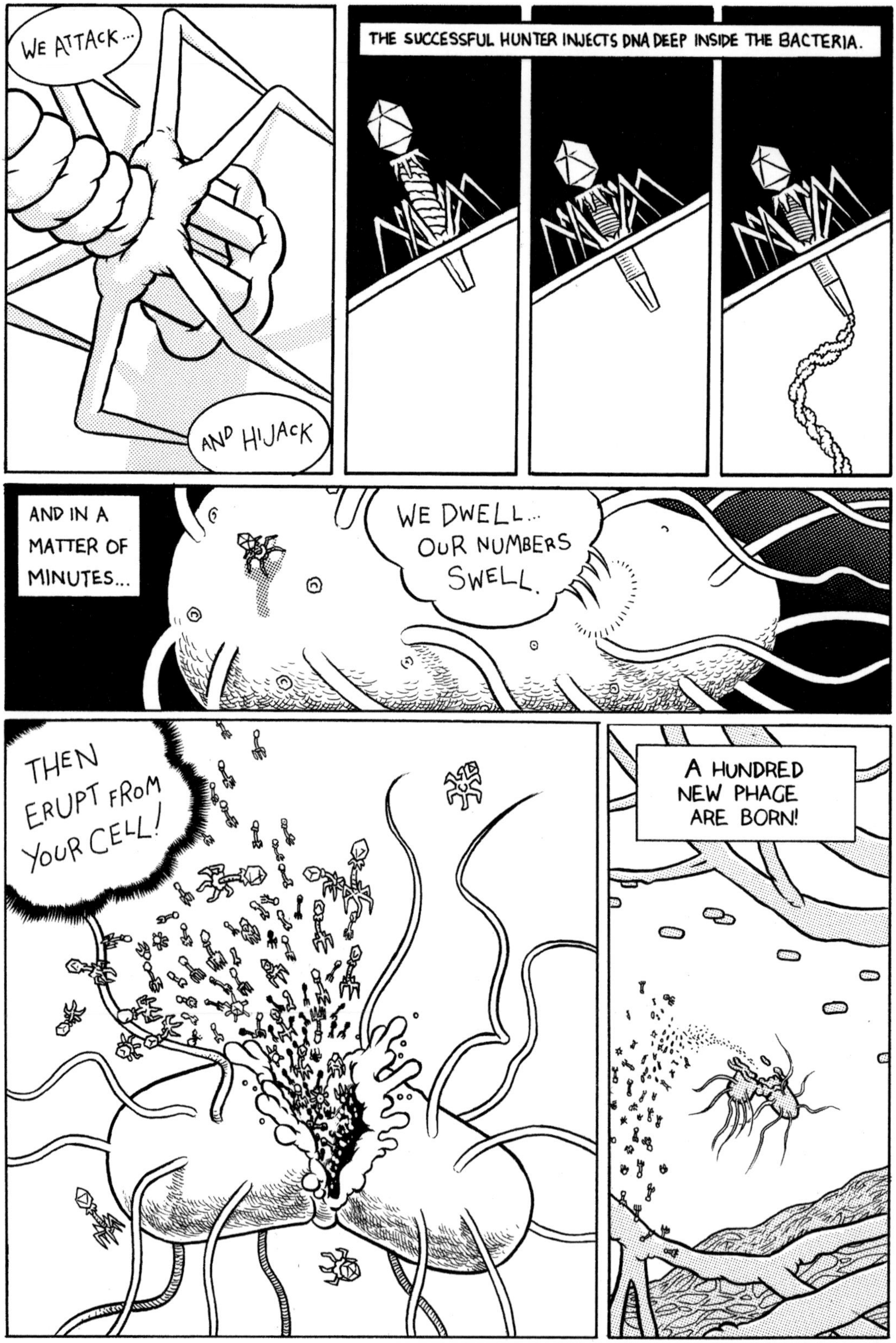
WE ATTACK...
AND HIJACK
THE SUCCESSFUL HUNTER INJECTS DNA DEEP INSIDE THE BACTERIA.
AND IN A MATTER OF MINUTES...
WE DWELL... OUR NUMBERS SWELL.
THEN ERUPT FROM YOUR CELL!
A HUNDRED NEW PHAGE ARE BORN!

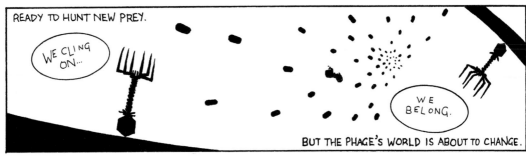

READY TO HUNT NEW PREY.

WE CLING ON...

WE BELONG.

BUT THE PHAGE'S WORLD IS ABOUT TO CHANGE.

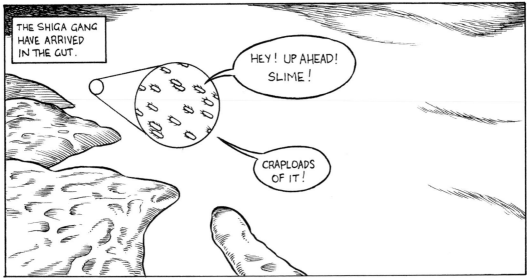

THE SHIGA GANG HAVE ARRIVED IN THE GUT.

HEY! UP AHEAD! SLIME!

CRAPLOADS OF IT!

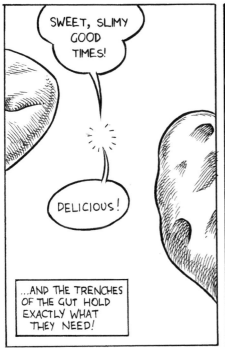

SWEET, SLIMY GOOD TIMES!

DELICIOUS!

...AND THE TRENCHES OF THE GUT HOLD EXACTLY WHAT THEY NEED!

I'M GONNA DIG ME INTO A TRENCH RIGHT NOW!

LET'S FIND OURSELVES SOMEWHERE TO BREED!

33

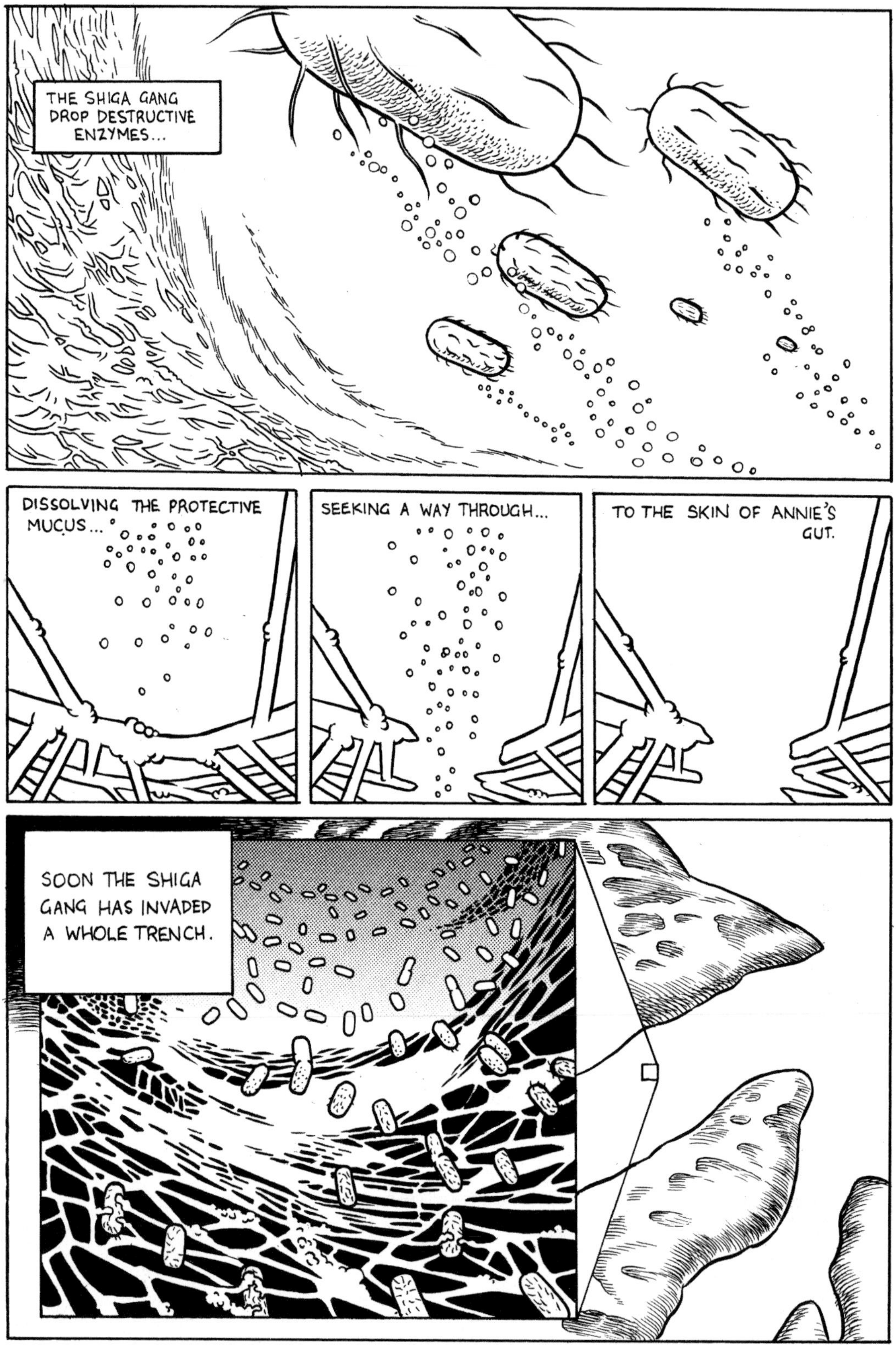
THE SHIGA GANG DROP DESTRUCTIVE ENZYMES...
DISSOLVING THE PROTECTIVE MUCUS...
SEEKING A WAY THROUGH...
TO THE SKIN OF ANNIE'S GUT.
SOON THE SHIGA GANG HAS INVADED A WHOLE TRENCH.

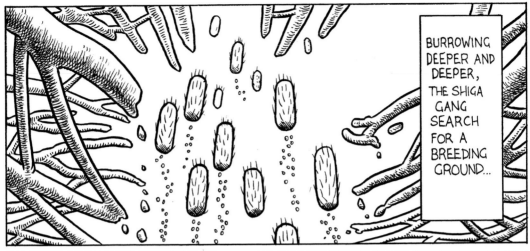

BURROWING DEEPER AND DEEPER, THE SHIGA GANG SEARCH FOR A BREEDING GROUND...

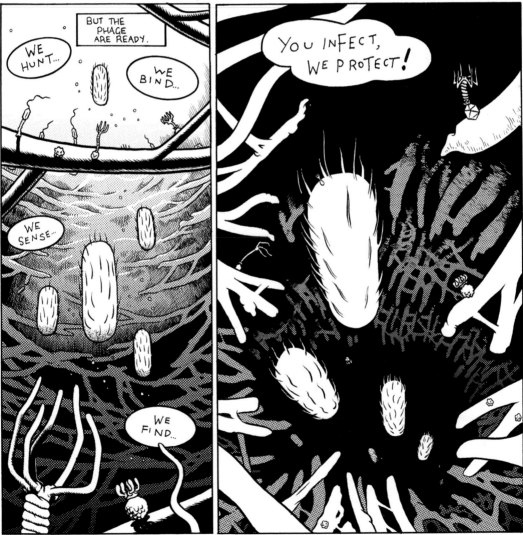

BUT THE PHAGE ARE READY.

WE HUNT...

WE BIND...

WE SENSE...

WE FIND...

YOU INFECT, WE PROTECT!

A SINGLE, TINY PODOPHAGE VENTURES OUT TO INFECT AN INVADING SHIGELLA.

ARE YOU SERIOUS!? GOOD LUCK, PUNY DUDE! YOU DON'T EVEN KNOW ME! HOW'RE YOU GONNA ATTACK ME!

WE HUNT FOR THE LOCK—THE WAY TO UNBLOCK!

WE ROLL, WE SEEK...

WE ARE STRONG, YOU ARE WEAK!

INCORRECT KEY... OUR PREY GOES FREE!

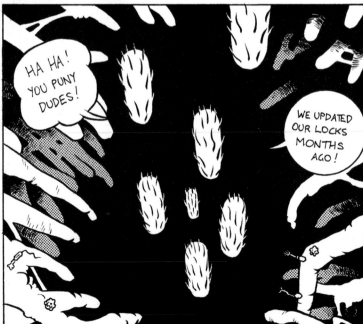

HA HA! YOU PUNY DUDES!

WE UPDATED OUR LOCKS MONTHS AGO!

WRONG SHAPE! OUR PREY ESCAPES!

BUT NONE OF THE PHAGE HAVE A KEY TO FIT THE SHIGA LOCK. THEY ARE HELPLESS.

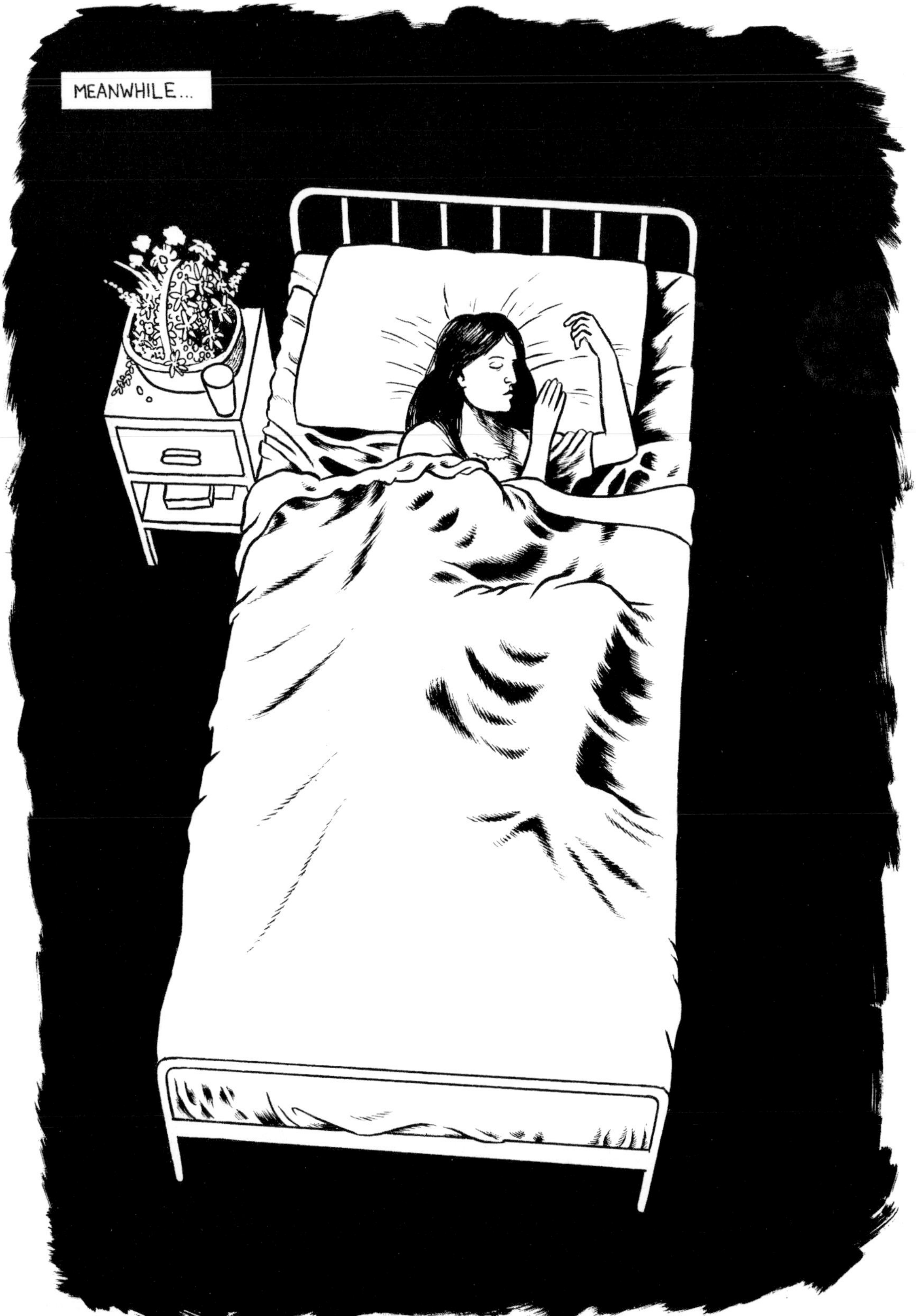
MEANWHILE...

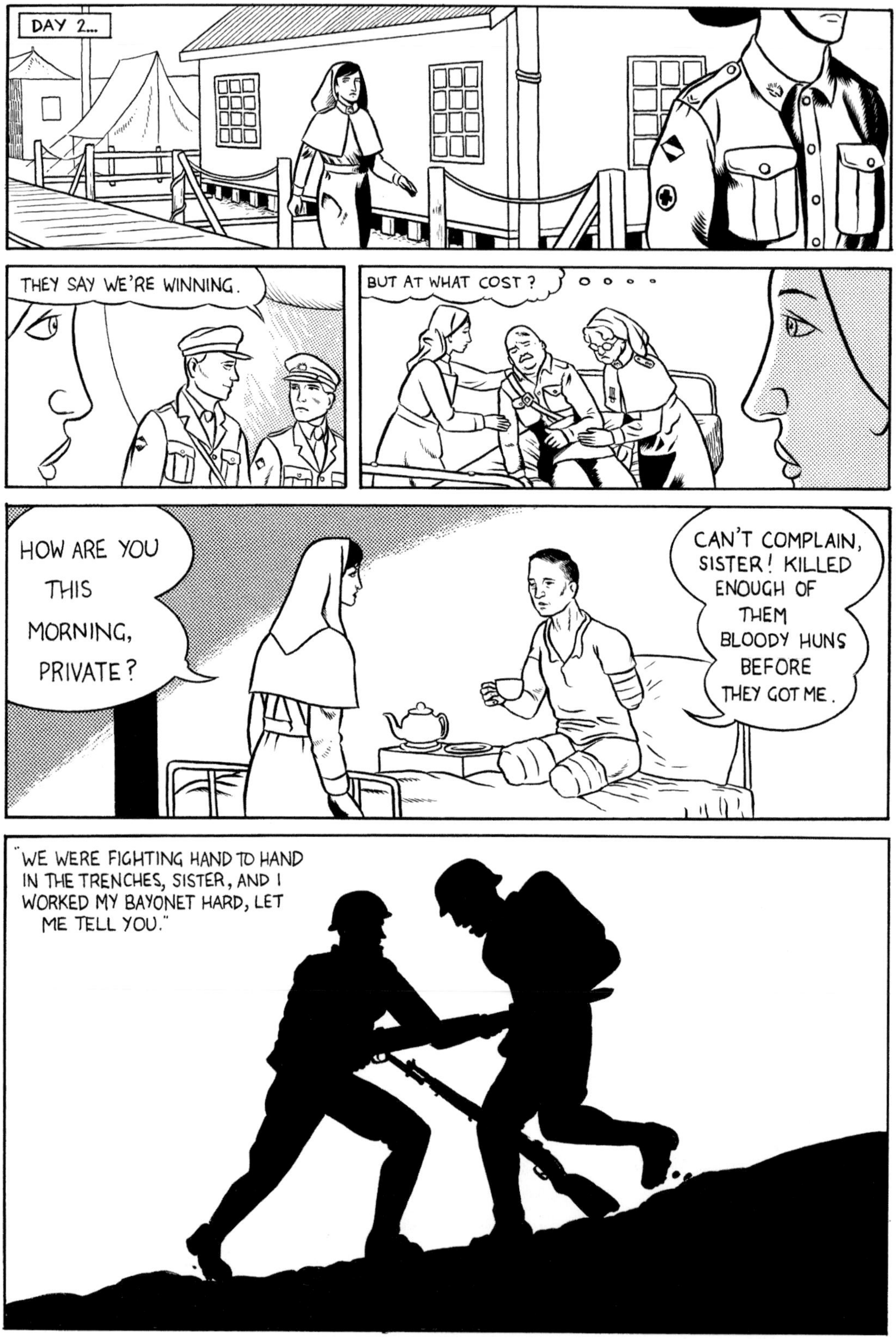
DAY 2...
THEY SAY WE'RE WINNING.
BUT AT WHAT COST?
HOW ARE YOU THIS MORNING, PRIVATE?
CAN'T COMPLAIN, SISTER! KILLED ENOUGH OF THEM BLOODY HUNS BEFORE THEY GOT ME.
"WE WERE FIGHTING HAND TO HAND IN THE TRENCHES, SISTER, AND I WORKED MY BAYONET HARD, LET ME TELL YOU."

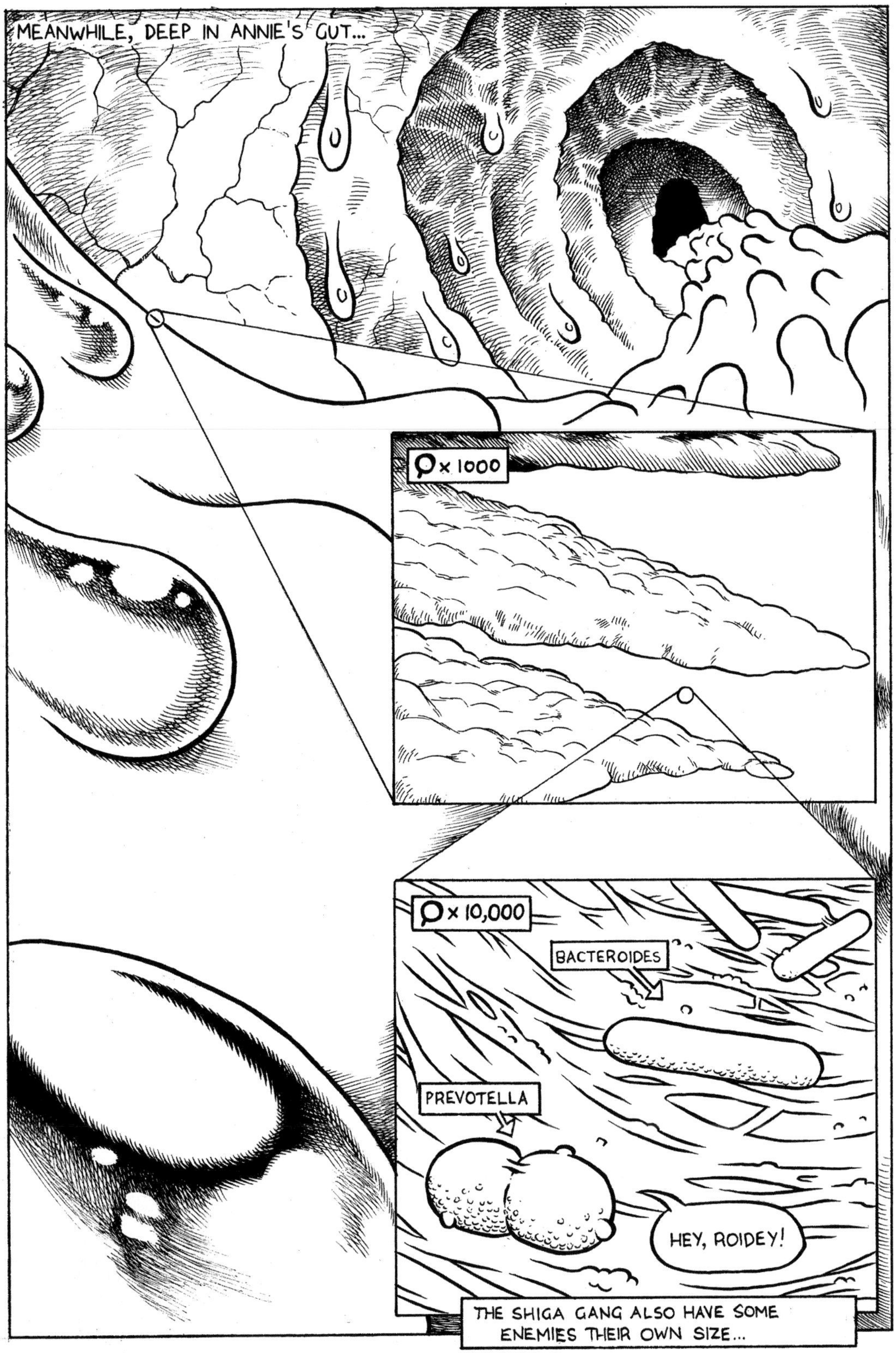
MEANWHILE, DEEP IN ANNIE'S GUT...
x 1000
x 10,000
BACTEROIDES
PREVOTELLA
HEY, ROIDEY!
THE SHIGA GANG ALSO HAVE SOME ENEMIES THEIR OWN SIZE...

I SPOT SOME INVADERS!

YOU'RE RIGHT, TELLA!

LET'S GET 'EM!

COME ON, GIRLS!

POP!

POP!

ROIDEY AND TELLA POP THEIR BAYONETS!

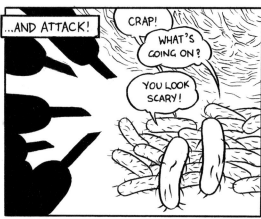

...AND ATTACK!

CRAP!

WHAT'S GOING ON?

YOU LOOK SCARY!

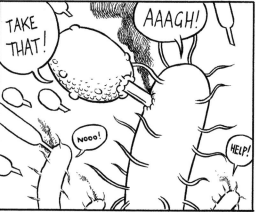

TAKE THAT!

AAAGH!

NOOO!

HELP!

MANY OF THE GANG ARE DESTROYED...

...BUT FARTHER UP THE TRENCH AND DEEP IN THE MUCUS, SOME SHIGA ARE SAFE.

40

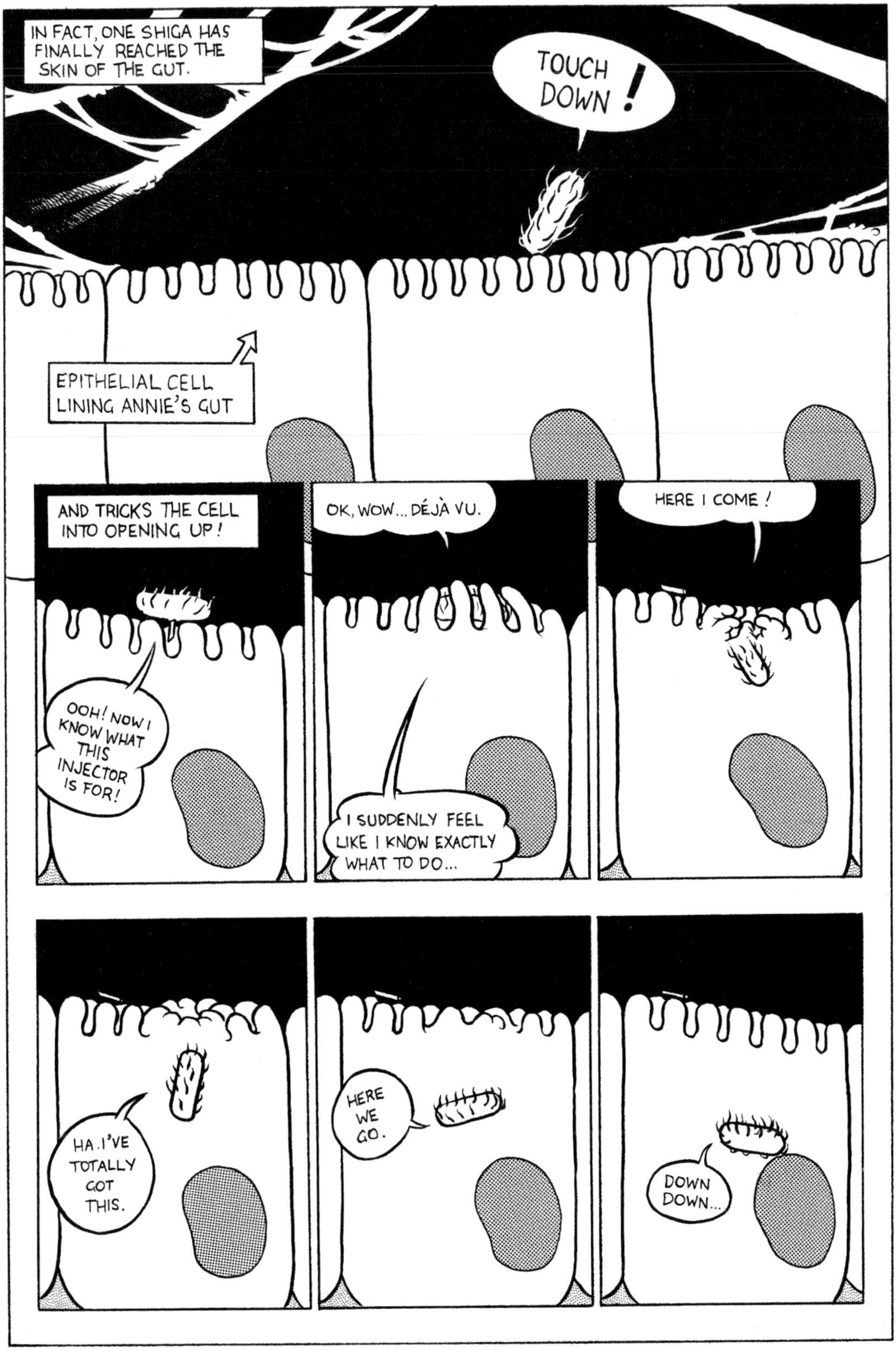

IN FACT, ONE SHIGA HAS FINALLY REACHED THE SKIN OF THE GUT.
TOUCH DOWN!
EPITHELIAL CELL LINING ANNIE'S GUT
AND TRICKS THE CELL INTO OPENING UP!
OOH! NOW I KNOW WHAT THIS INJECTOR IS FOR!
OK, WOW... DÉJÀ VU.
I SUDDENLY FEEL LIKE I KNOW EXACTLY WHAT TO DO...
HERE I COME!
HA. I'VE TOTALLY GOT THIS.
HERE WE GO.
DOWN DOWN...

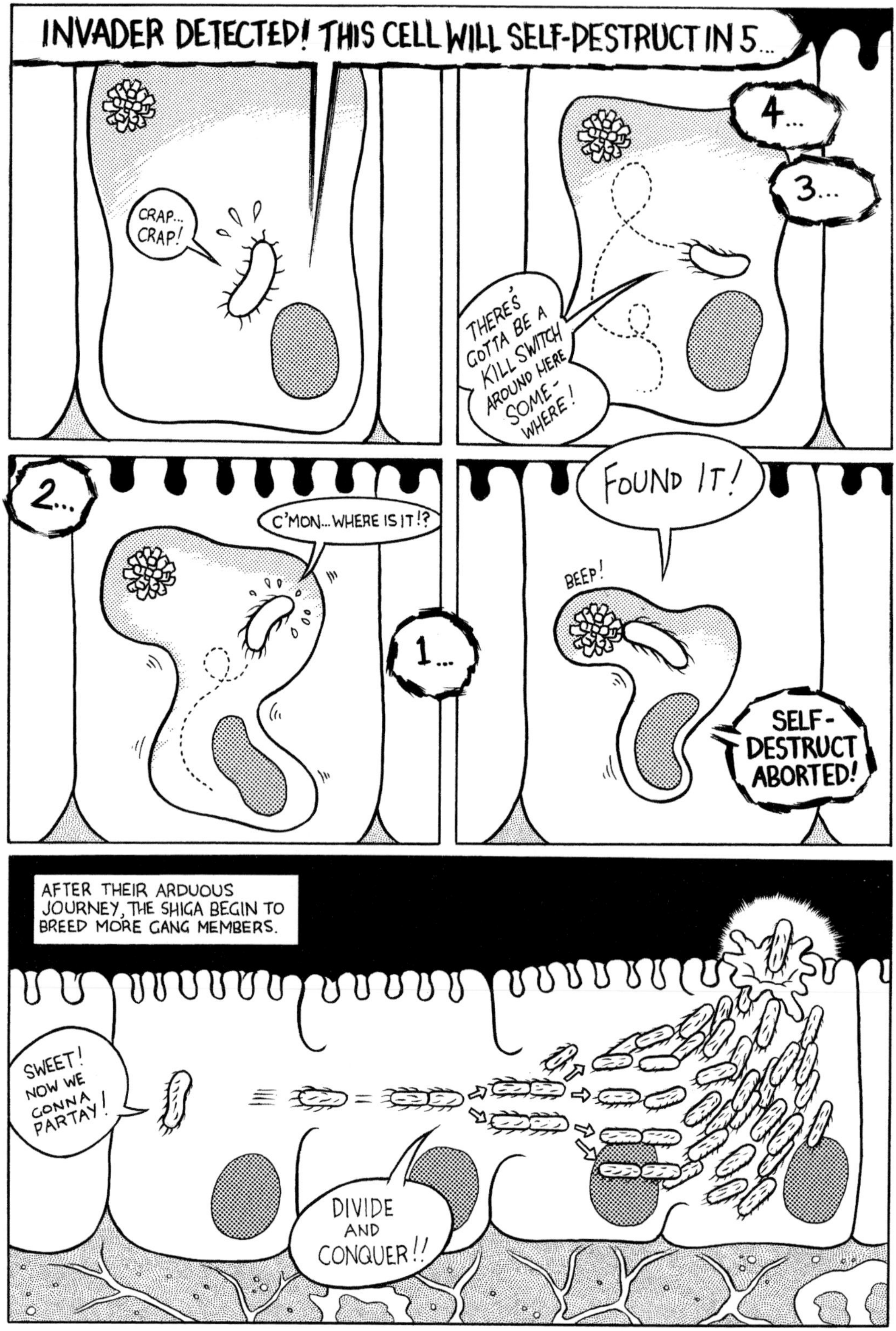
INVADER DETECTED! THIS CELL WILL SELF-DESTRUCT IN 5...
CRAP... CRAP!
4...
3...
THERE'S GOTTA BE A KILL SWITCH AROUND HERE SOME-WHERE!
2...
C'MON... WHERE IS IT!?
1...
FOUND IT!
BEEP!
SELF-DESTRUCT ABORTED!
AFTER THEIR ARDUOUS JOURNEY, THE SHIGA BEGIN TO BREED MORE GANG MEMBERS.
SWEET! NOW WE GONNA PARTAY!
DIVIDE AND CONQUER!!

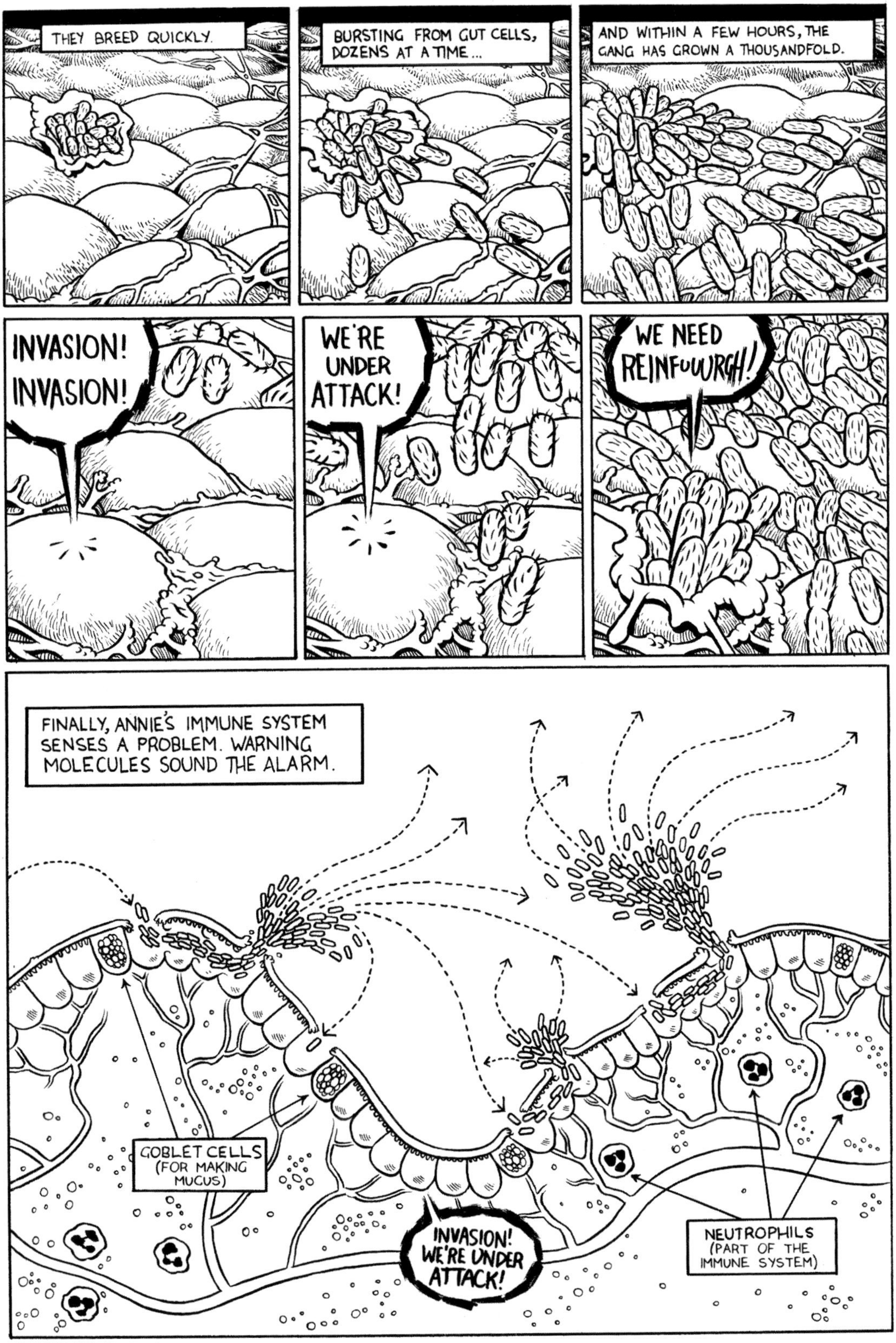
THEY BREED QUICKLY.
BURSTING FROM GUT CELLS, DOZENS AT A TIME...
AND WITHIN A FEW HOURS, THE GANG HAS GROWN A THOUSANDFOLD.
INVASION! INVASION!
WE'RE UNDER ATTACK!
WE NEED REINFUUURGH!
FINALLY, ANNIE'S IMMUNE SYSTEM SENSES A PROBLEM. WARNING MOLECULES SOUND THE ALARM.
GOBLET CELLS (FOR MAKING MUCUS)
INVASION! WE'RE UNDER ATTACK!
NEUTROPHILS (PART OF THE IMMUNE SYSTEM)

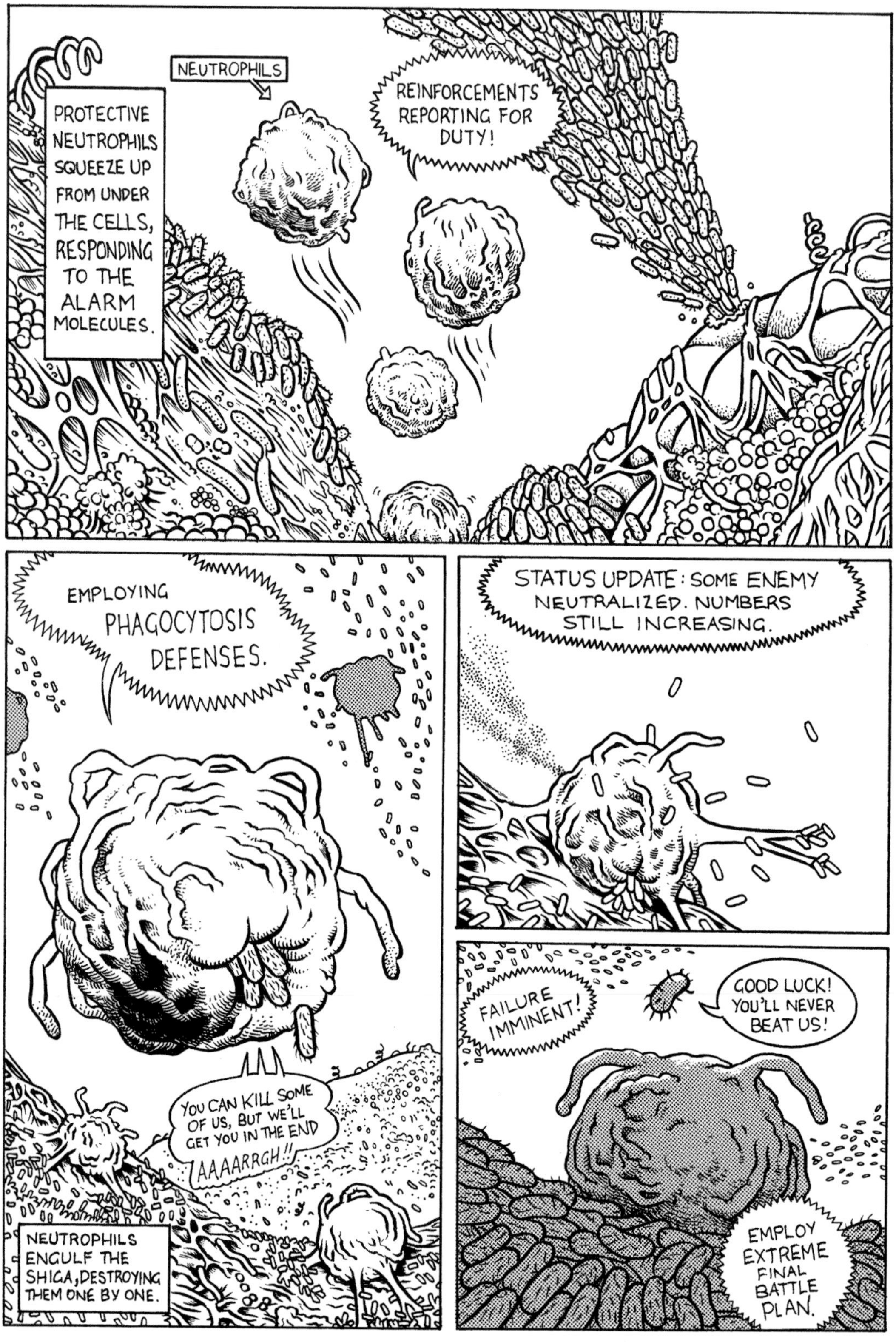
PROTECTIVE NEUTROPHILS SQUEEZE UP FROM UNDER THE CELLS, RESPONDING TO THE ALARM MOLECULES.
NEUTROPHILS
REINFORCEMENTS REPORTING FOR DUTY!
EMPLOYING PHAGOCYTOSIS DEFENSES.
YOU CAN KILL SOME OF US, BUT WE'LL GET YOU IN THE END
AAAARRGH!!
NEUTROPHILS ENGULF THE SHIGA, DESTROYING THEM ONE BY ONE.
STATUS UPDATE: SOME ENEMY NEUTRALIZED. NUMBERS STILL INCREASING.
FAILURE IMMINENT!
GOOD LUCK! YOU'LL NEVER BEAT US!
EMPLOY EXTREME FINAL BATTLE PLAN.

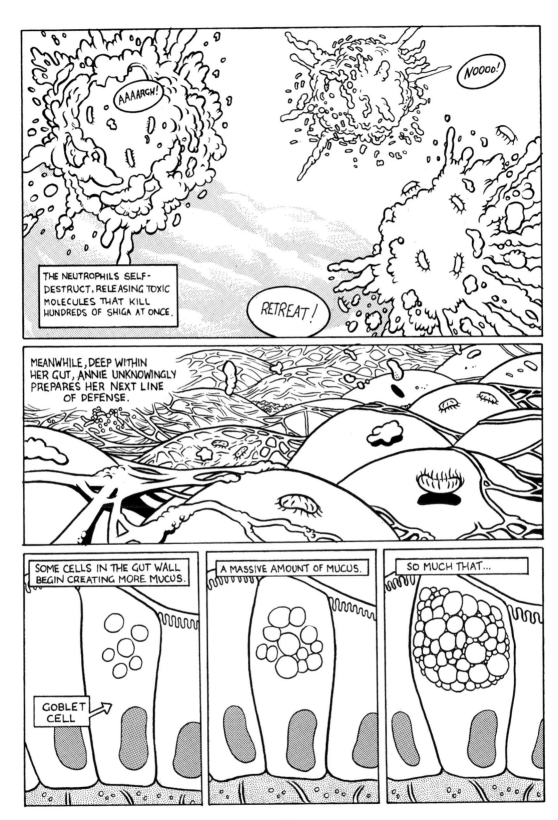

AAAARGH!

NOOOO!

THE NEUTROPHILS SELF-DESTRUCT, RELEASING TOXIC MOLECULES THAT KILL HUNDREDS OF SHIGA AT ONCE.

RETREAT!

MEANWHILE, DEEP WITHIN HER GUT, ANNIE UNKNOWINGLY PREPARES HER NEXT LINE OF DEFENSE.

SOME CELLS IN THE GUT WALL BEGIN CREATING MORE MUCUS.

GOBLET CELL

A MASSIVE AMOUNT OF MUCUS.

SO MUCH THAT...

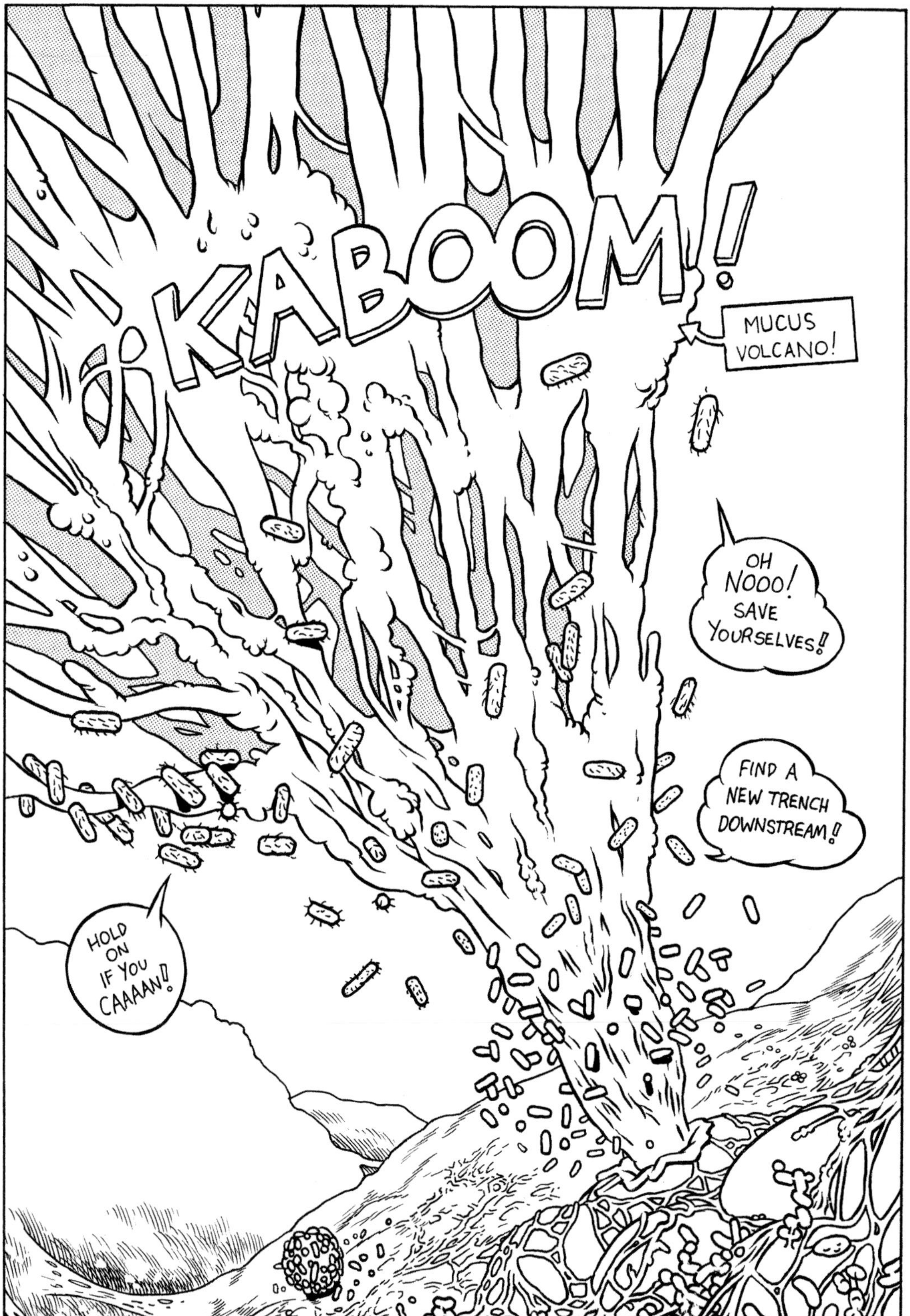
KABOOM!
MUCUS VOLCANO!
OH NOOO! SAVE YOURSELVES!
FIND A NEW TRENCH DOWNSTREAM!
HOLD ON IF YOU CAAAAN!

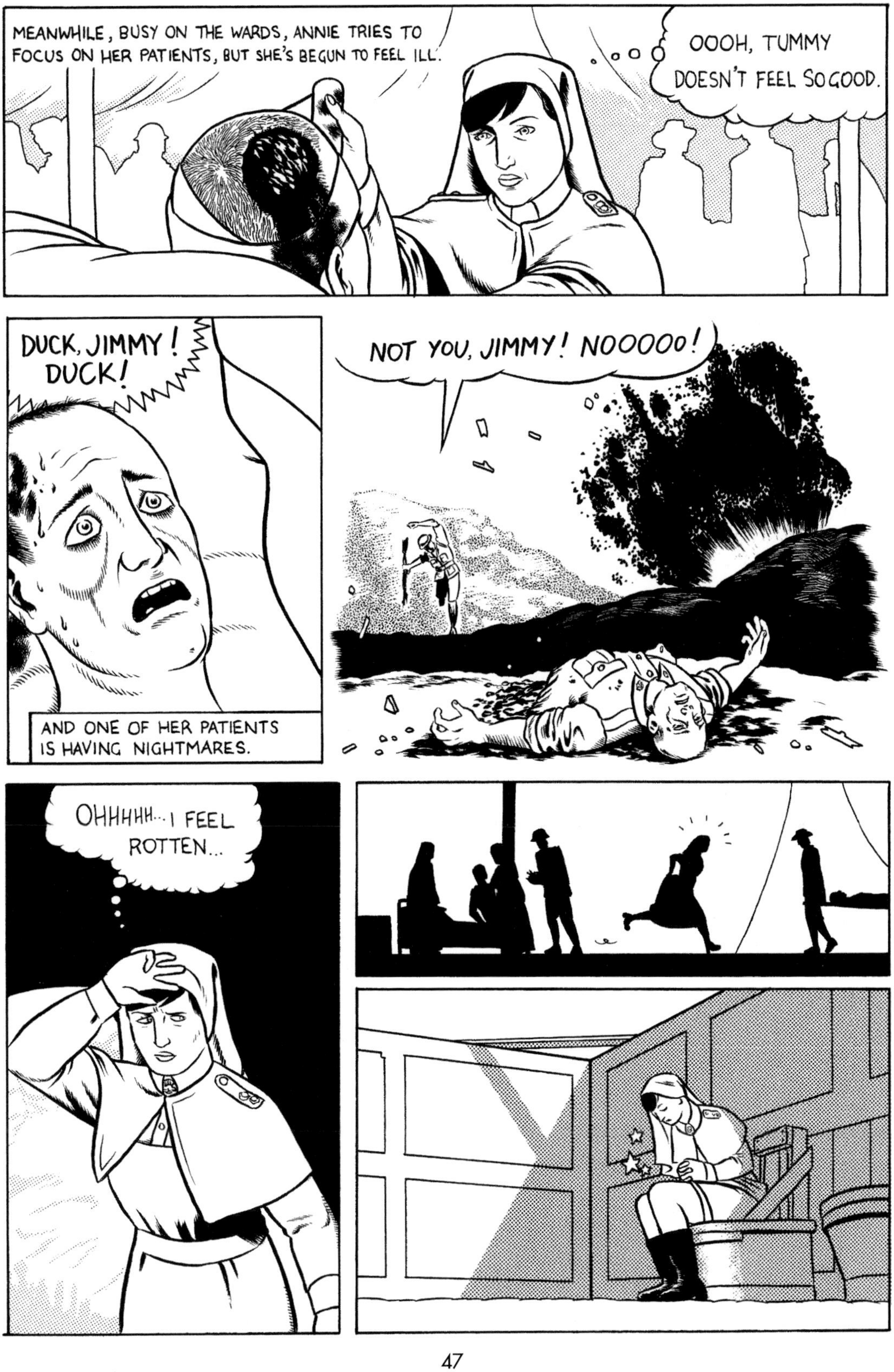
MEANWHILE, BUSY ON THE WARDS, ANNIE TRIES TO FOCUS ON HER PATIENTS, BUT SHE'S BEGUN TO FEEL ILL.
OOOH, TUMMY DOESN'T FEEL SO GOOD.
DUCK, JIMMY! DUCK!
AND ONE OF HER PATIENTS IS HAVING NIGHTMARES.
NOT YOU, JIMMY! NOOOOO!
OHHHHH... I FEEL ROTTEN...

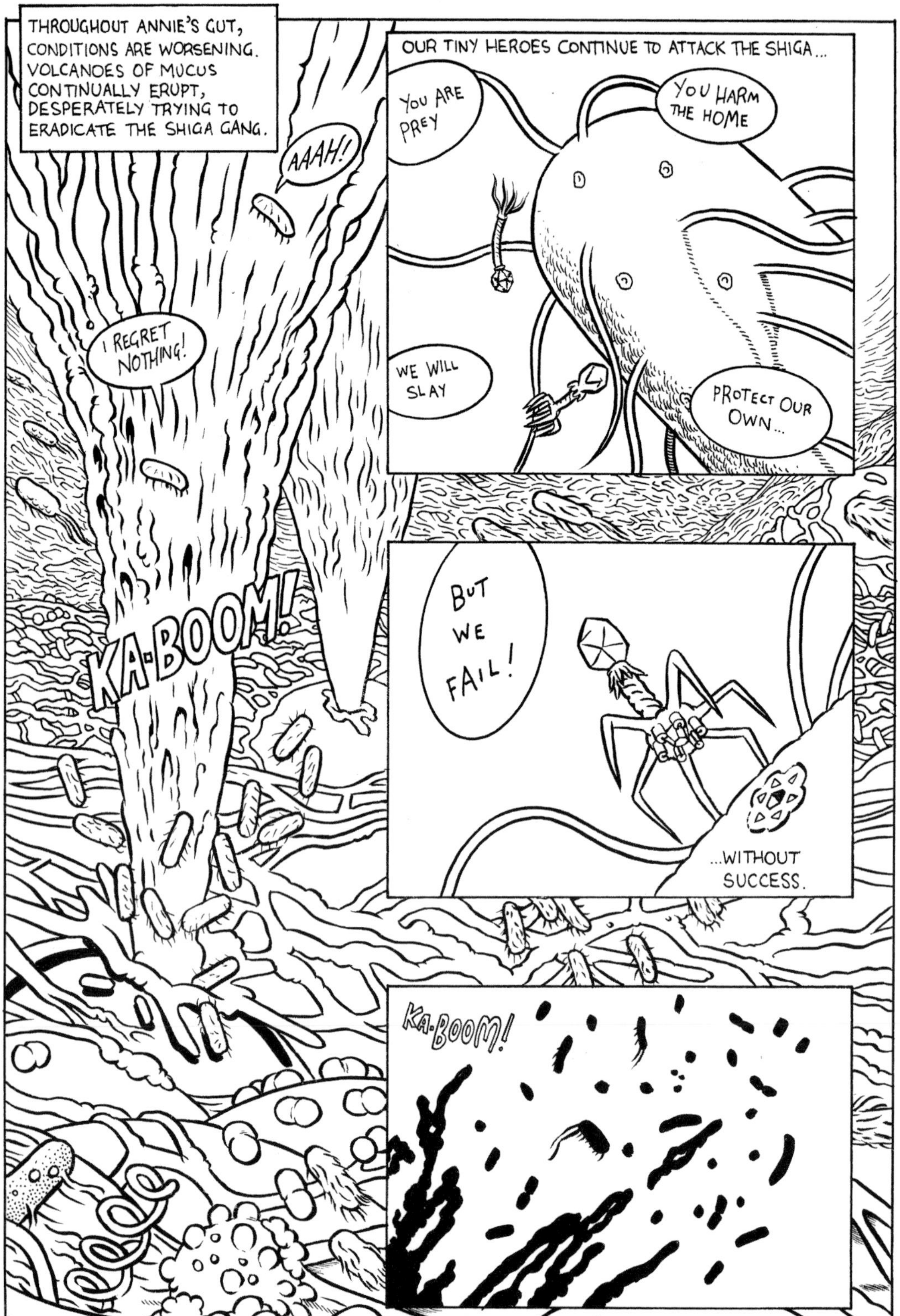
THROUGHOUT ANNIE'S GUT, CONDITIONS ARE WORSENING. VOLCANOES OF MUCUS CONTINUALLY ERUPT, DESPERATELY TRYING TO ERADICATE THE SHIGA GANG.
AAAH!
I REGRET NOTHING!
KA-BOOM!
OUR TINY HEROES CONTINUE TO ATTACK THE SHIGA...
YOU ARE PREY
YOU HARM THE HOME
WE WILL SLAY
PROTECT OUR OWN...
BUT WE FAIL!
...WITHOUT SUCCESS.
KA-BOOM!

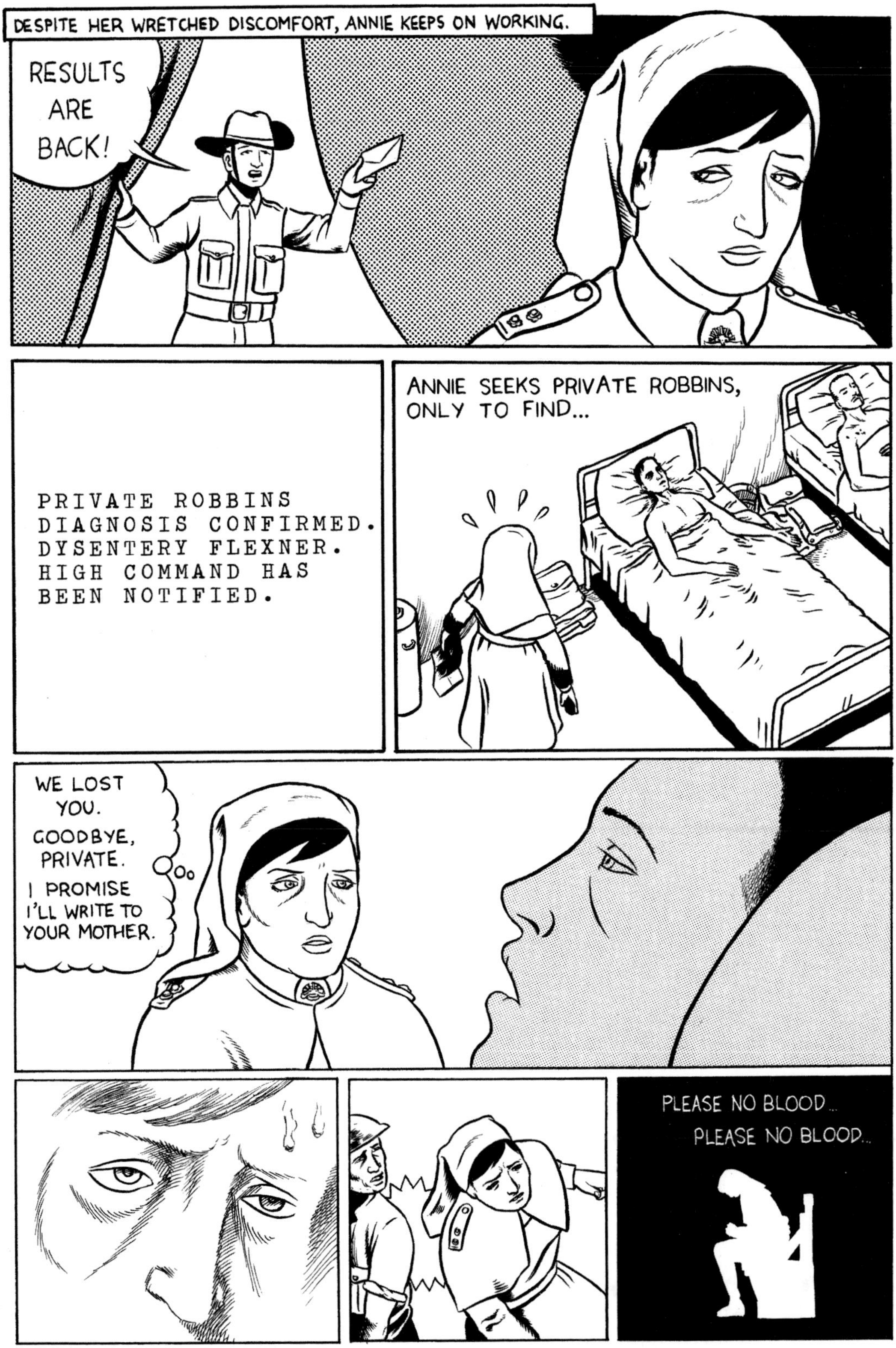
DESPITE HER WRETCHED DISCOMFORT, ANNIE KEEPS ON WORKING.
RESULTS ARE BACK!
PRIVATE ROBBINS DIAGNOSIS CONFIRMED. DYSENTERY FLEXNER. HIGH COMMAND HAS BEEN NOTIFIED.
ANNIE SEEKS PRIVATE ROBBINS, ONLY TO FIND...
WE LOST YOU. GOODBYE, PRIVATE. I PROMISE I'LL WRITE TO YOUR MOTHER.
PLEASE NO BLOOD... PLEASE NO BLOOD...

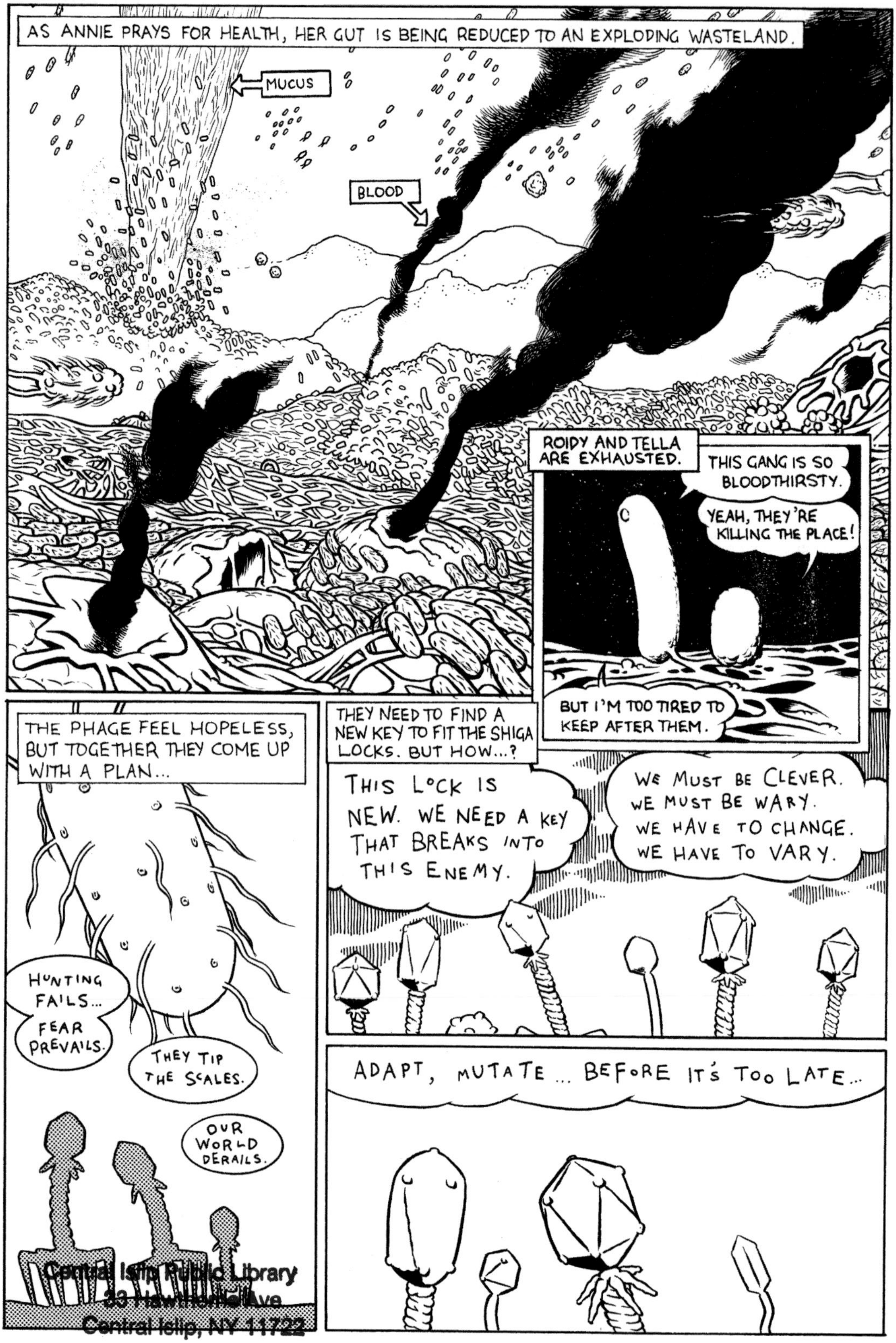

AS ANNIE PRAYS FOR HEALTH, HER GUT IS BEING REDUCED TO AN EXPLODING WASTELAND.
MUCUS
BLOOD
ROIDY AND TELLA ARE EXHAUSTED.
THIS GANG IS SO BLOODTHIRSTY.
YEAH, THEY'RE KILLING THE PLACE!
BUT I'M TOO TIRED TO KEEP AFTER THEM.
THE PHAGE FEEL HOPELESS, BUT TOGETHER THEY COME UP WITH A PLAN...
HUNTING FAILS...
FEAR PREVAILS.
THEY TIP THE SCALES.
OUR WORLD DERAILS.
THEY NEED TO FIND A NEW KEY TO FIT THE SHIGA LOCKS. BUT HOW...?
THIS LOCK IS NEW. WE NEED A KEY THAT BREAKS INTO THIS ENEMY.
WE MUST BE CLEVER. WE MUST BE WARY. WE HAVE TO CHANGE. WE HAVE TO VARY.
ADAPT, MUTATE ... BEFORE IT'S TOO LATE...

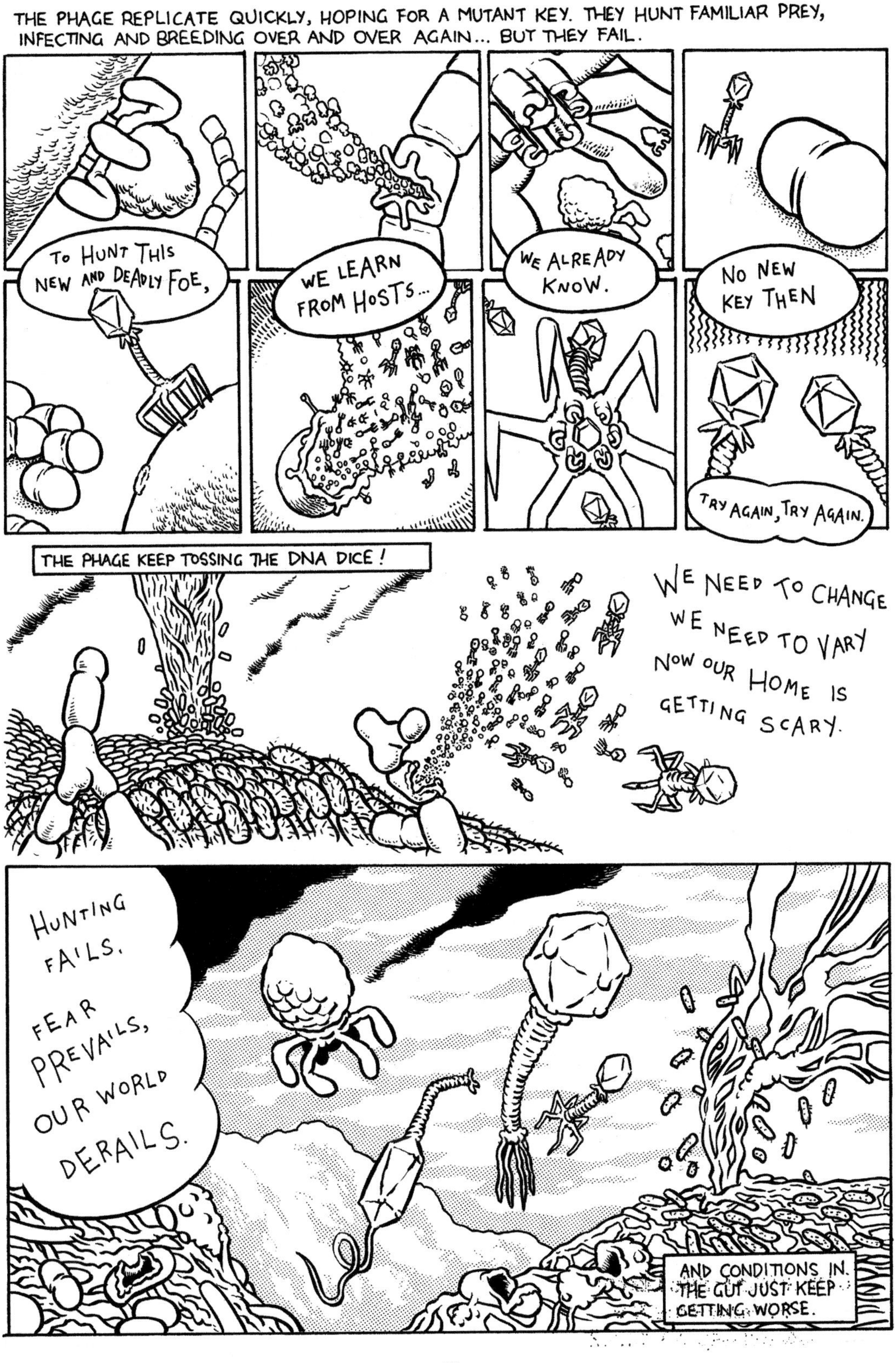
THE PHAGE REPLICATE QUICKLY, HOPING FOR A MUTANT KEY. THEY HUNT FAMILIAR PREY, INFECTING AND BREEDING OVER AND OVER AGAIN... BUT THEY FAIL.
TO HUNT THIS NEW AND DEADLY FOE,
WE LEARN FROM HOSTS...
WE ALREADY KNOW.
NO NEW KEY THEN
TRY AGAIN, TRY AGAIN.
THE PHAGE KEEP TOSSING THE DNA DICE!
WE NEED TO CHANGE
WE NEED TO VARY
NOW OUR HOME IS GETTING SCARY.
HUNTING FAILS.
FEAR PREVAILS,
OUR WORLD DERAILS.
AND CONDITIONS IN THE GUT JUST KEEP GETTING WORSE.

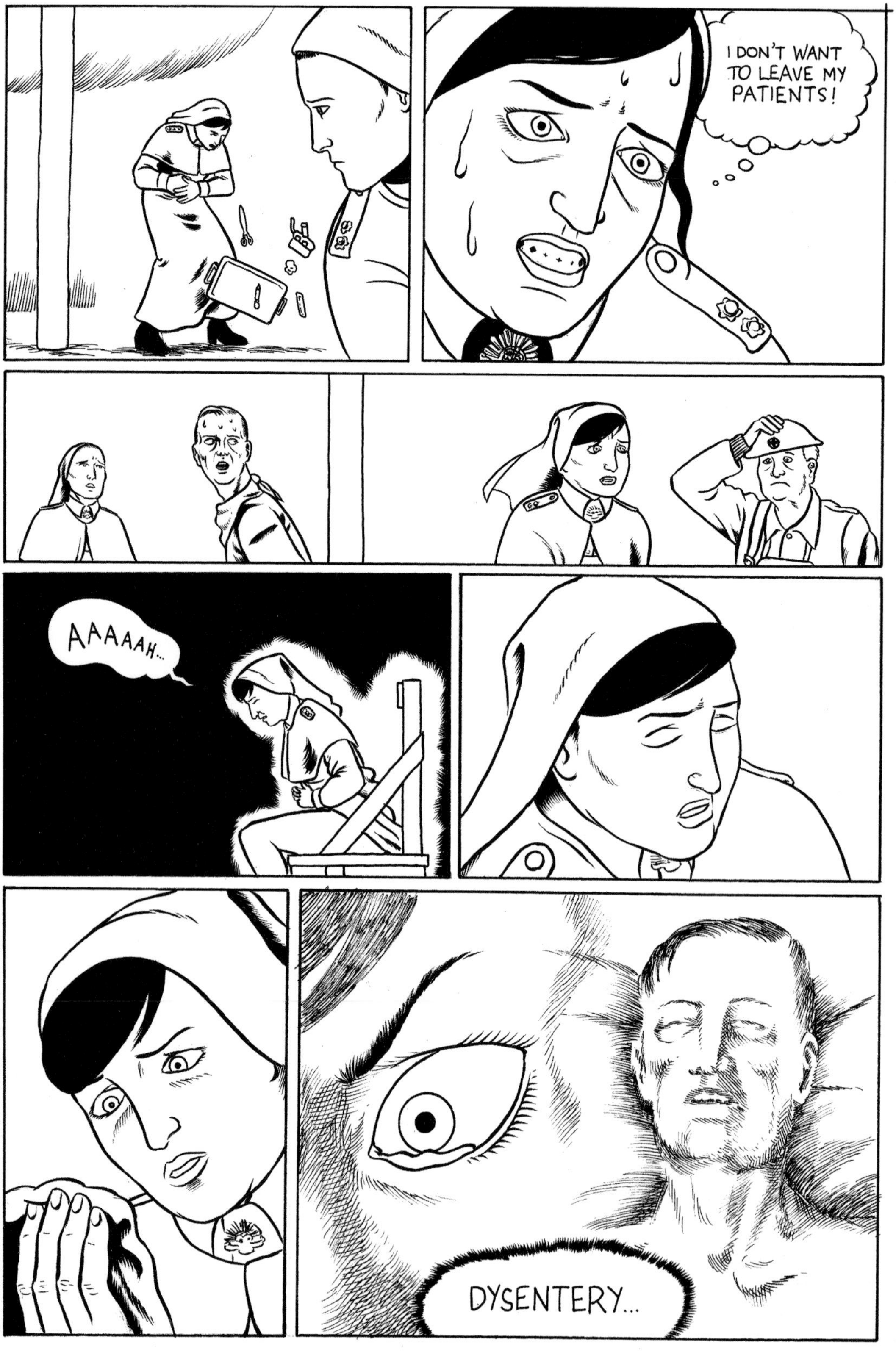
I DON'T WANT TO LEAVE MY PATIENTS!
AAAAAH...
DYSENTERY...

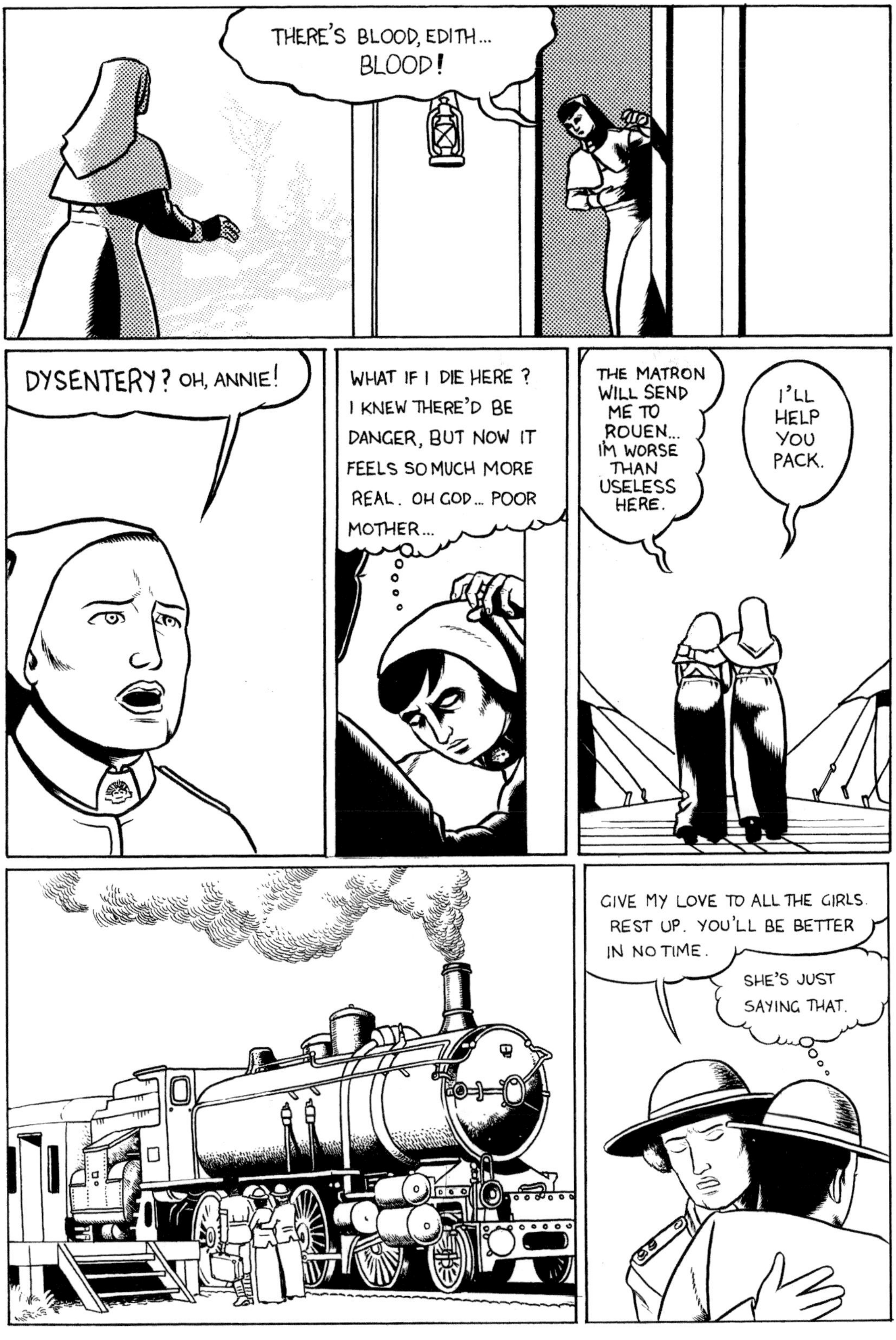

THERE'S BLOOD, EDITH... BLOOD!
DYSENTERY? OH, ANNIE!
WHAT IF I DIE HERE? I KNEW THERE'D BE DANGER, BUT NOW IT FEELS SO MUCH MORE REAL. OH GOD... POOR MOTHER...
THE MATRON WILL SEND ME TO ROUEN... I'M WORSE THAN USELESS HERE.
I'LL HELP YOU PACK.
GIVE MY LOVE TO ALL THE GIRLS. REST UP. YOU'LL BE BETTER IN NO TIME.
SHE'S JUST SAYING THAT.

WELCOME TO THE SICK SISTERS HOSPITAL.

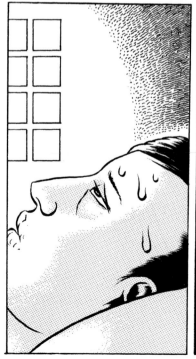

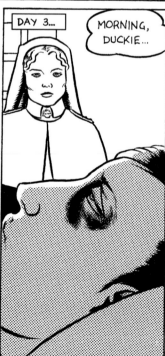

DAY 3...

MORNING, DUCKIE...

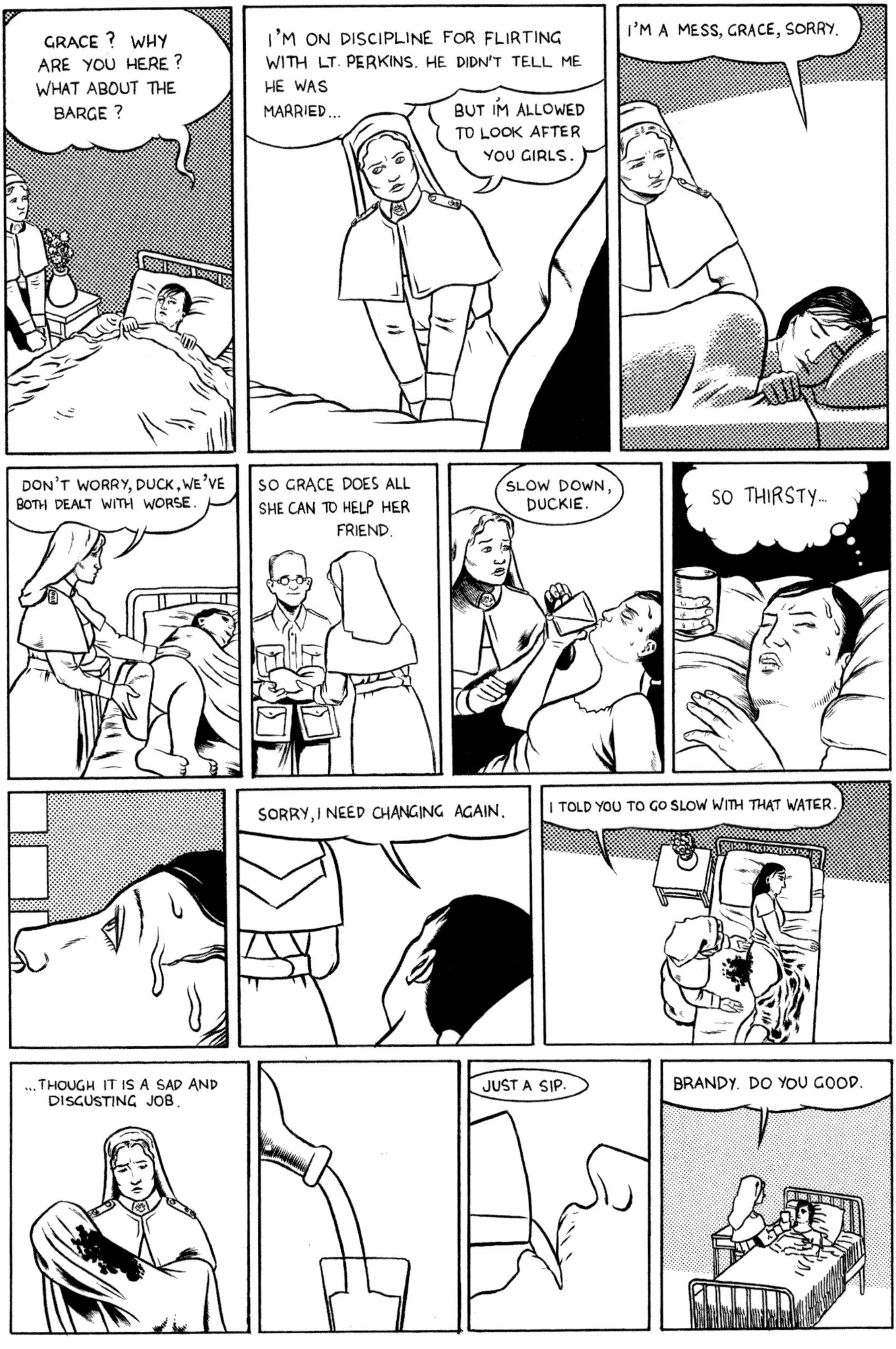

GRACE? WHY ARE YOU HERE? WHAT ABOUT THE BARGE?
I'M ON DISCIPLINE FOR FLIRTING WITH LT. PERKINS. HE DIDN'T TELL ME HE WAS MARRIED...
BUT I'M ALLOWED TO LOOK AFTER YOU GIRLS.
I'M A MESS, GRACE, SORRY.
DON'T WORRY, DUCK, WE'VE BOTH DEALT WITH WORSE.
SO GRACE DOES ALL SHE CAN TO HELP HER FRIEND.
SLOW DOWN, DUCKIE.
SO THIRSTY...
SORRY, I NEED CHANGING AGAIN.
I TOLD YOU TO GO SLOW WITH THAT WATER.
...THOUGH IT IS A SAD AND DISGUSTING JOB.
JUST A SIP.
BRANDY. DO YOU GOOD.

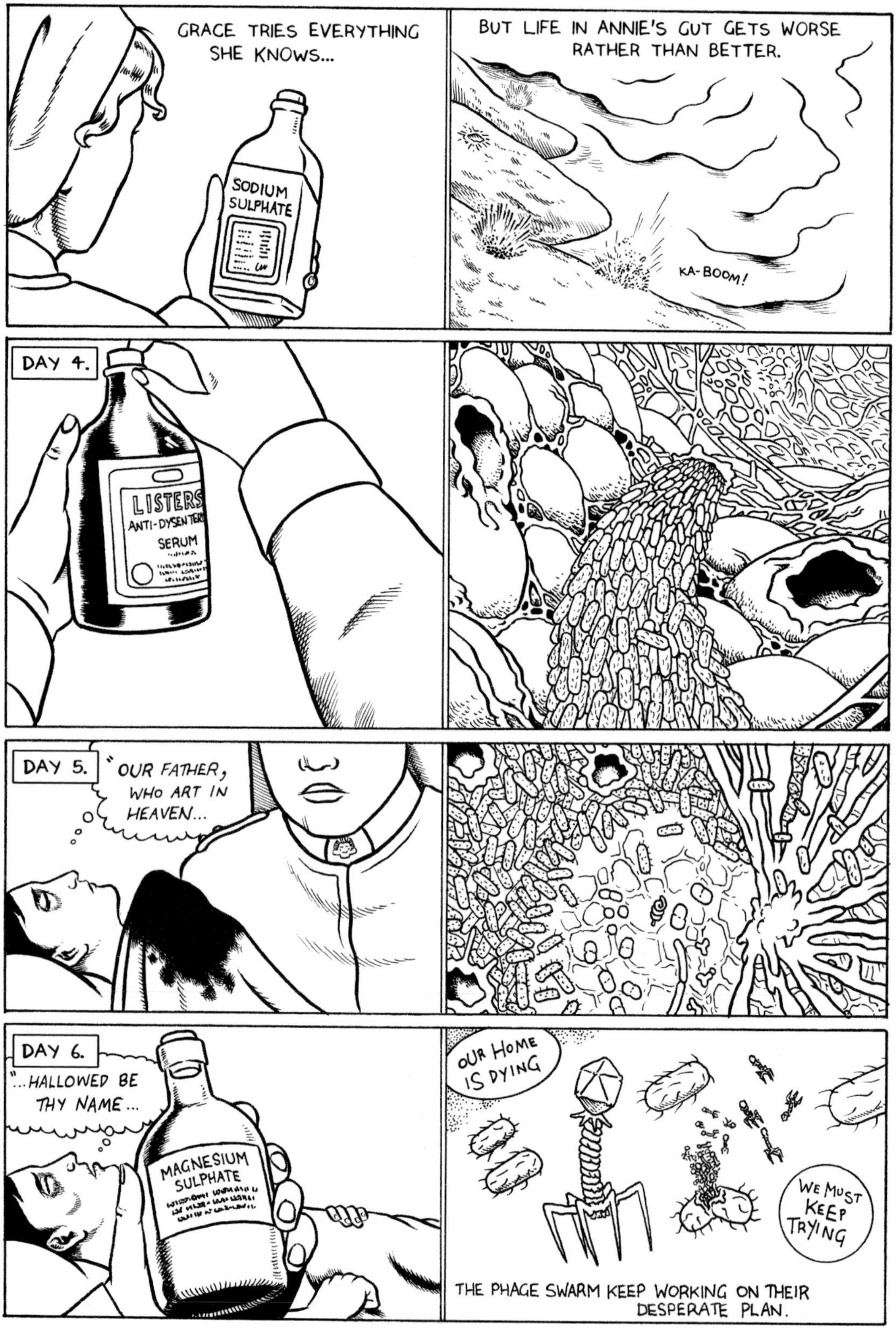
GRACE TRIES EVERYTHING SHE KNOWS...
SODIUM SULPHATE
BUT LIFE IN ANNIE'S GUT GETS WORSE RATHER THAN BETTER.
KA-BOOM!
DAY 4.
LISTERS
ANTI-DYSENTER
SERUM
DAY 5.
"OUR FATHER, WHO ART IN HEAVEN...
DAY 6.
"...HALLOWED BE THY NAME...
MAGNESIUM SULPHATE
OUR HOME IS DYING
WE MUST KEEP TRYING
THE PHAGE SWARM KEEP WORKING ON THEIR DESPERATE PLAN.

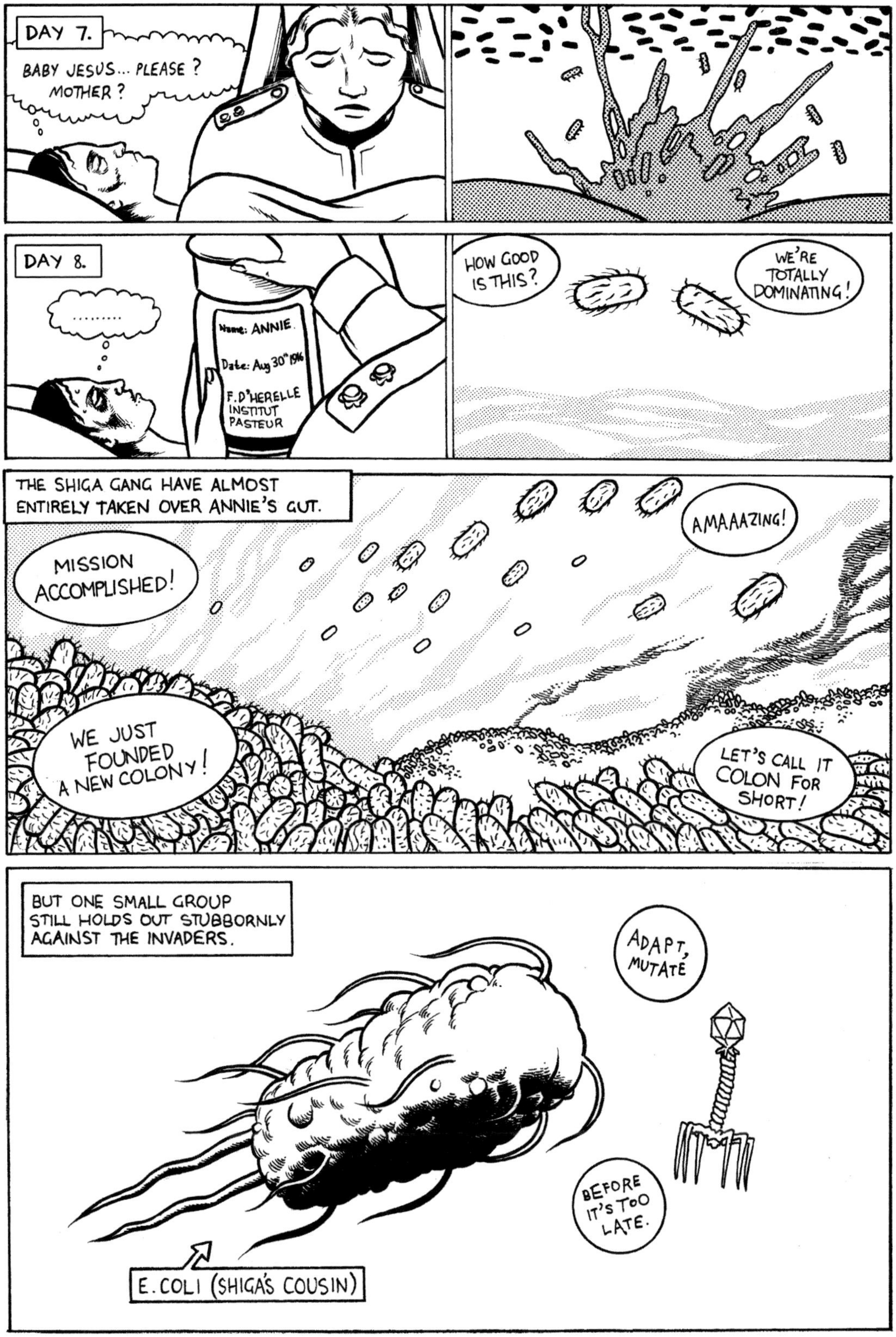
DAY 7.
BABY JESUS... PLEASE? MOTHER?
DAY 8.
....
Name: ANNIE
Date: Aug 30th 1916
F. D'HERELLE INSTITUT PASTEUR
HOW GOOD IS THIS?
WE'RE TOTALLY DOMINATING!
THE SHIGA GANG HAVE ALMOST ENTIRELY TAKEN OVER ANNIE'S GUT.
MISSION ACCOMPLISHED!
AMAAAZING!
WE JUST FOUNDED A NEW COLONY!
LET'S CALL IT COLON FOR SHORT!
BUT ONE SMALL GROUP STILL HOLDS OUT STUBBORNLY AGAINST THE INVADERS.
ADAPT, MUTATE
BEFORE IT'S TOO LATE.
E. COLI (SHIGA'S COUSIN)

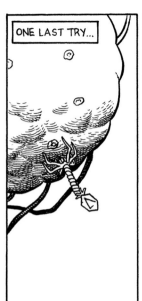

ONE LAST TRY...

BIND, MUTATE... BEFORE IT'S TOO LATE.

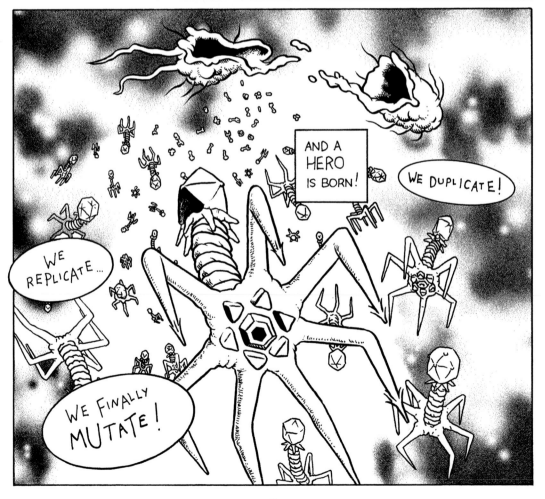

AND A HERO IS BORN!

WE DUPLICATE!

WE REPLICATE...

WE FINALLY MUTATE!

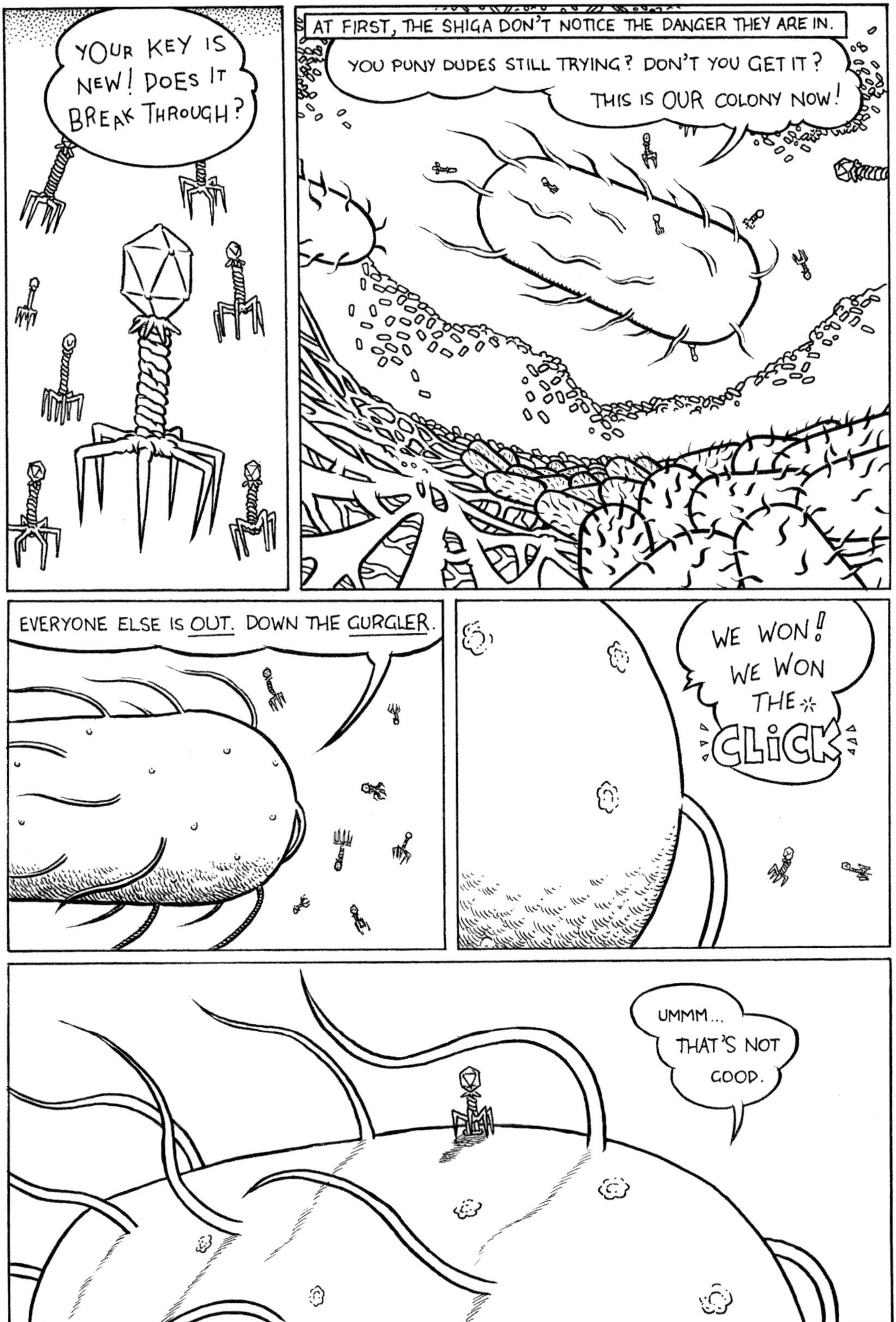

YOUR KEY IS NEW! DOES IT BREAK THROUGH?
AT FIRST, THE SHIGA DON'T NOTICE THE DANGER THEY ARE IN.
YOU PUNY DUDES STILL TRYING? DON'T YOU GET IT? THIS IS OUR COLONY NOW!
EVERYONE ELSE IS OUT. DOWN THE GURGLER.
WE WON! WE WON THE CLICK
UMMM... THAT'S NOT GOOD.

NOT GOOD AT ALL...

OUR HERO'S KEY FITS PERFECTLY. INTO THE SHIGA LOCK.

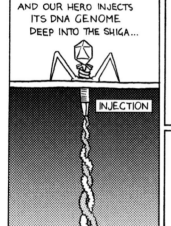

AND OUR HERO INJECTS ITS DNA GENOME DEEP INTO THE SHIGA...

INJECTION

THE DNA ROLLS INTO A CIRCLE...

HIJACKS THE ENTIRE SHIGA CELL...

CIRCULARIZATION

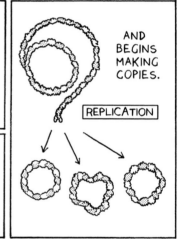

AND BEGINS MAKING COPIES.

REPLICATION

UM... GUYS...

A LITTLE HELP?

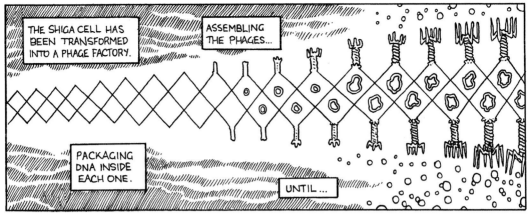

THE SHIGA CELL HAS BEEN TRANSFORMED INTO A PHAGE FACTORY.

ASSEMBLING THE PHAGES...

PACKAGING DNA INSIDE EACH ONE.

UNTIL ...

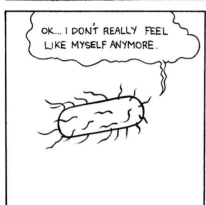

OK... I DON'T REALLY FEEL LIKE MYSELF ANYMORE.

THE SHIGA IS PACKED FULL OF PHAGES.

ITS MEMBRANE BEGINS TO DISSOLVE.

AAAAARGGHBLURGH

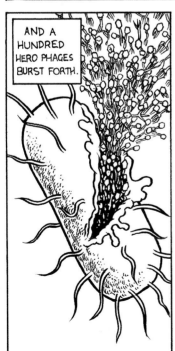

AND A HUNDRED HERO PHAGES BURST FORTH.

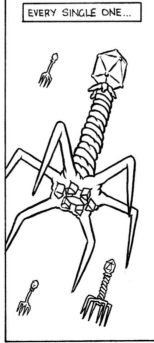

EVERY SINGLE ONE...

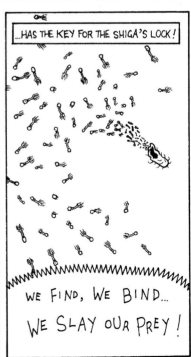

...HAS THE KEY FOR THE SHIGA'S LOCK!

WE FIND, WE BIND...
WE SLAY OUR PREY!

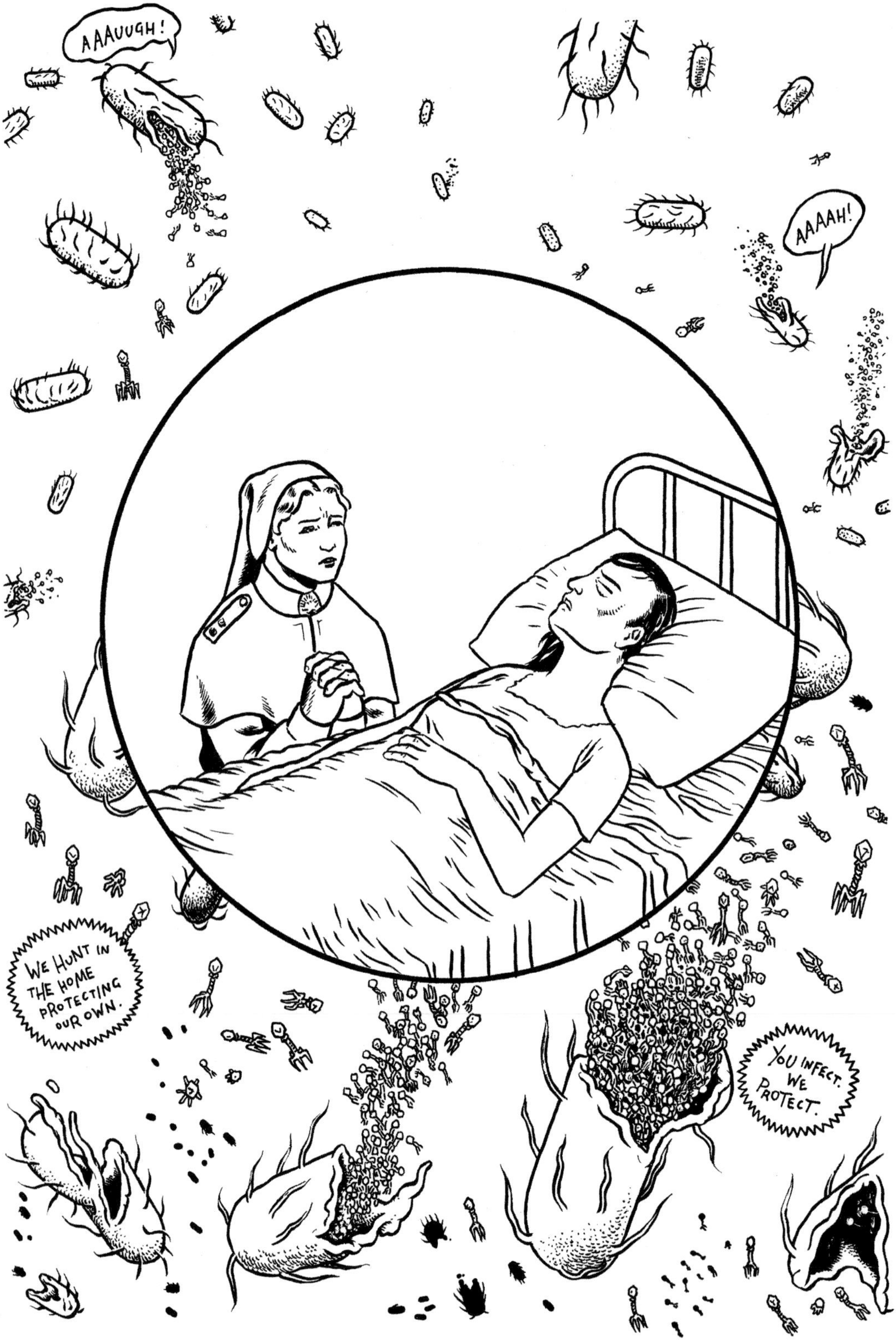
AAAUUGH!
AAAAH!
WE HUNT IN THE HOME PROTECTING OUR OWN.
YOU INFECT. WE PROTECT.

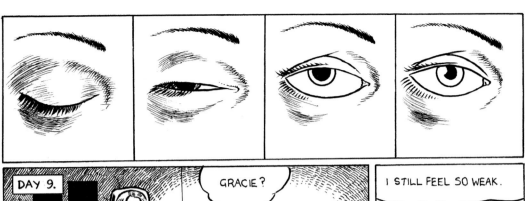

DAY 9.

GRACIE?

WELL, YOUR FEVER'S DOWN.

I STILL FEEL SO WEAK.

YOU'RE MUCH BETTER THAN YOU WERE. YOU COULD HAVE DIED YOU KNOW, DUCKIE. NOTHING I GAVE YOU WAS HELPING.

YOU MUST HAVE BEEN TERRIFIED.

YES. BUT THEN SUDDENLY YOU JUST RALLIED.

AND NOW HERE YOU ARE!

I SUPPOSE THE HUMAN BODY IS A STRANGE AND WONDERFUL THING.

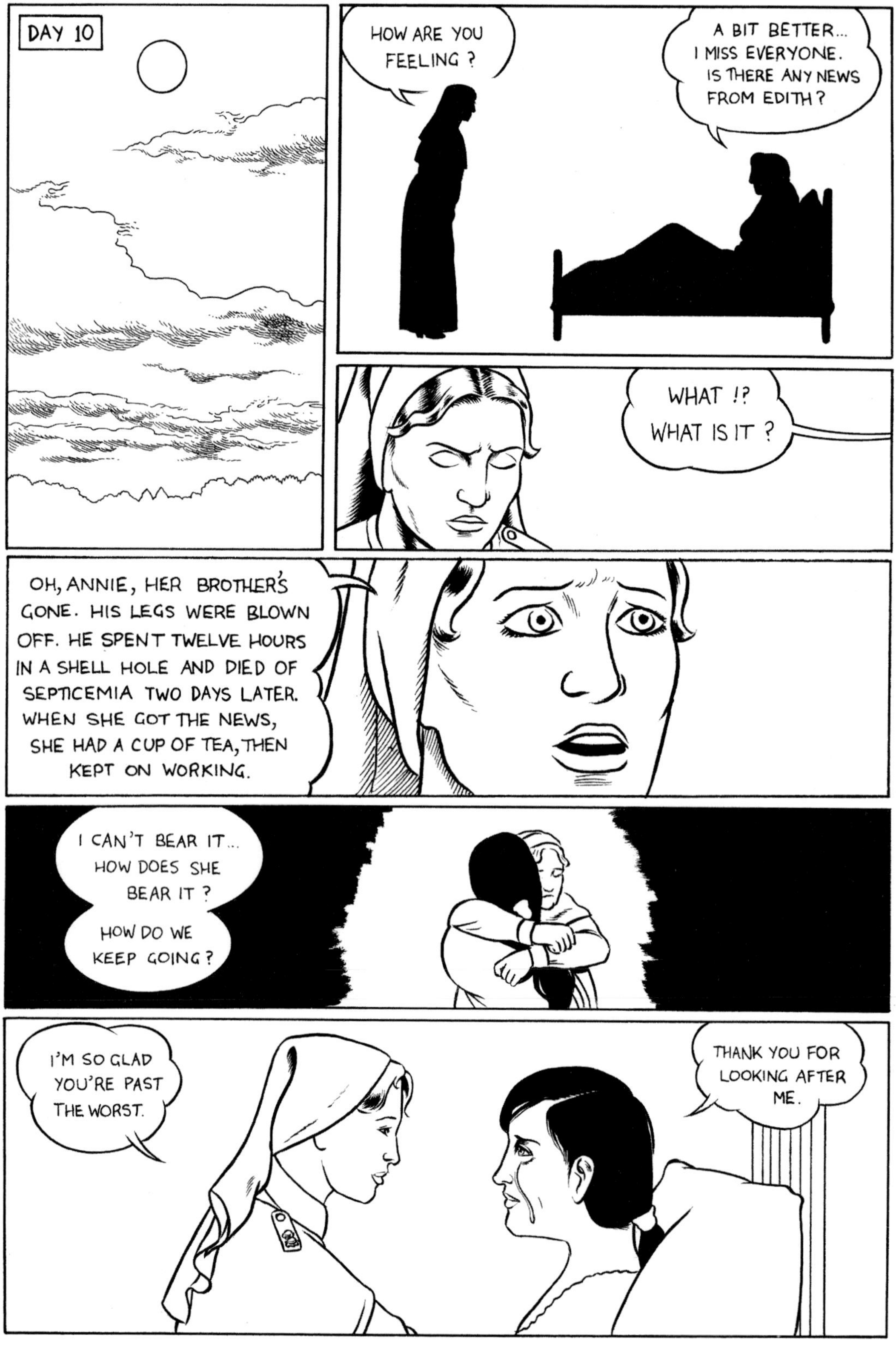
DAY 10
HOW ARE YOU FEELING ?
A BIT BETTER... I MISS EVERYONE. IS THERE ANY NEWS FROM EDITH ?
WHAT !? WHAT IS IT ?
OH, ANNIE, HER BROTHER'S GONE. HIS LEGS WERE BLOWN OFF. HE SPENT TWELVE HOURS IN A SHELL HOLE AND DIED OF SEPTICEMIA TWO DAYS LATER. WHEN SHE GOT THE NEWS, SHE HAD A CUP OF TEA, THEN KEPT ON WORKING.
I CAN'T BEAR IT... HOW DOES SHE BEAR IT ?
HOW DO WE KEEP GOING ?
I'M SO GLAD YOU'RE PAST THE WORST.
THANK YOU FOR LOOKING AFTER ME.

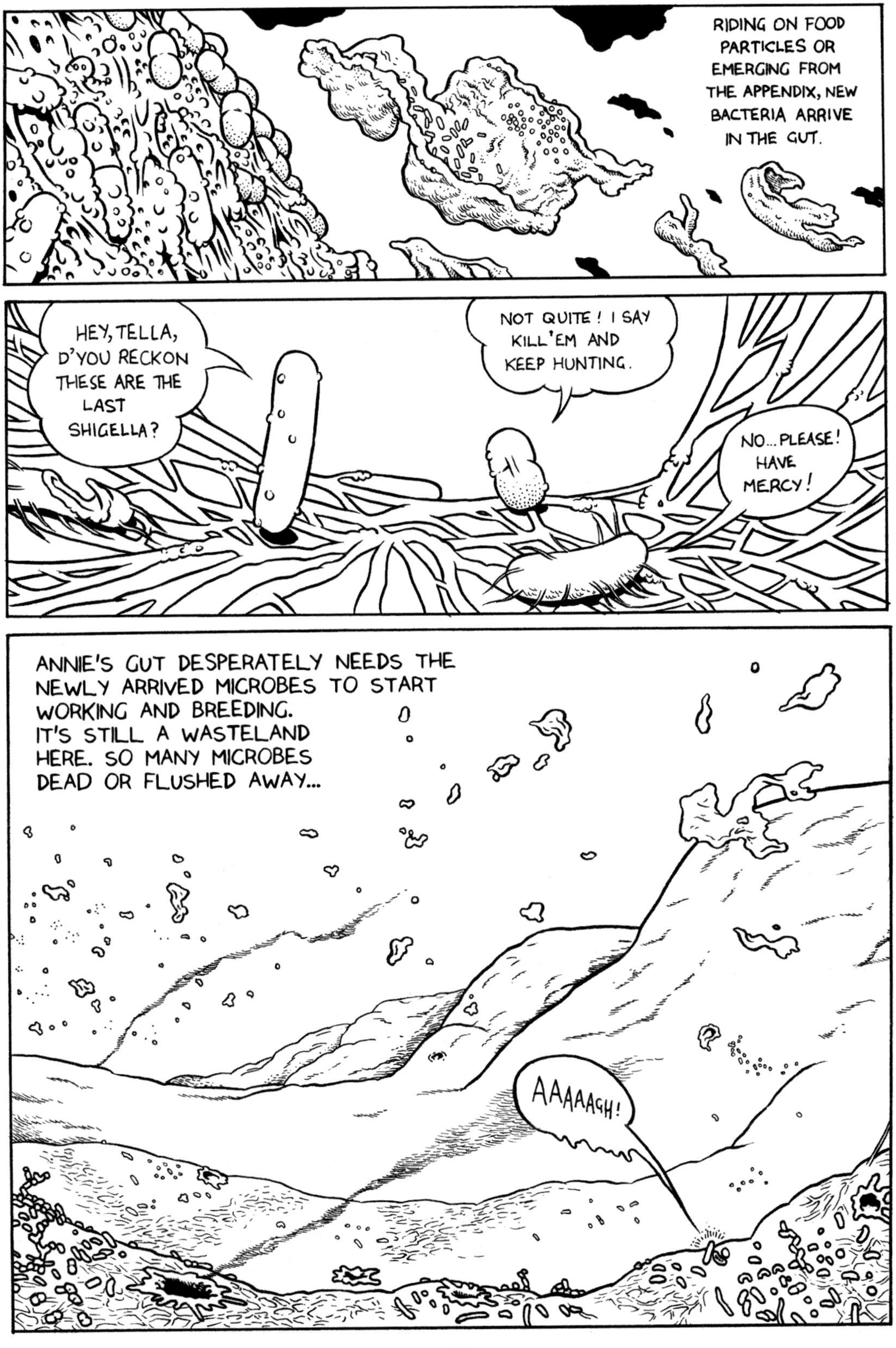

RIDING ON FOOD PARTICLES OR EMERGING FROM THE APPENDIX, NEW BACTERIA ARRIVE IN THE GUT.
HEY, TELLA, D'YOU RECKON THESE ARE THE LAST SHIGELLA?
NOT QUITE! I SAY KILL'EM AND KEEP HUNTING.
NO... PLEASE! HAVE MERCY!
ANNIE'S GUT DESPERATELY NEEDS THE NEWLY ARRIVED MICROBES TO START WORKING AND BREEDING. IT'S STILL A WASTELAND HERE. SO MANY MICROBES DEAD OR FLUSHED AWAY...
AAAAAGH!

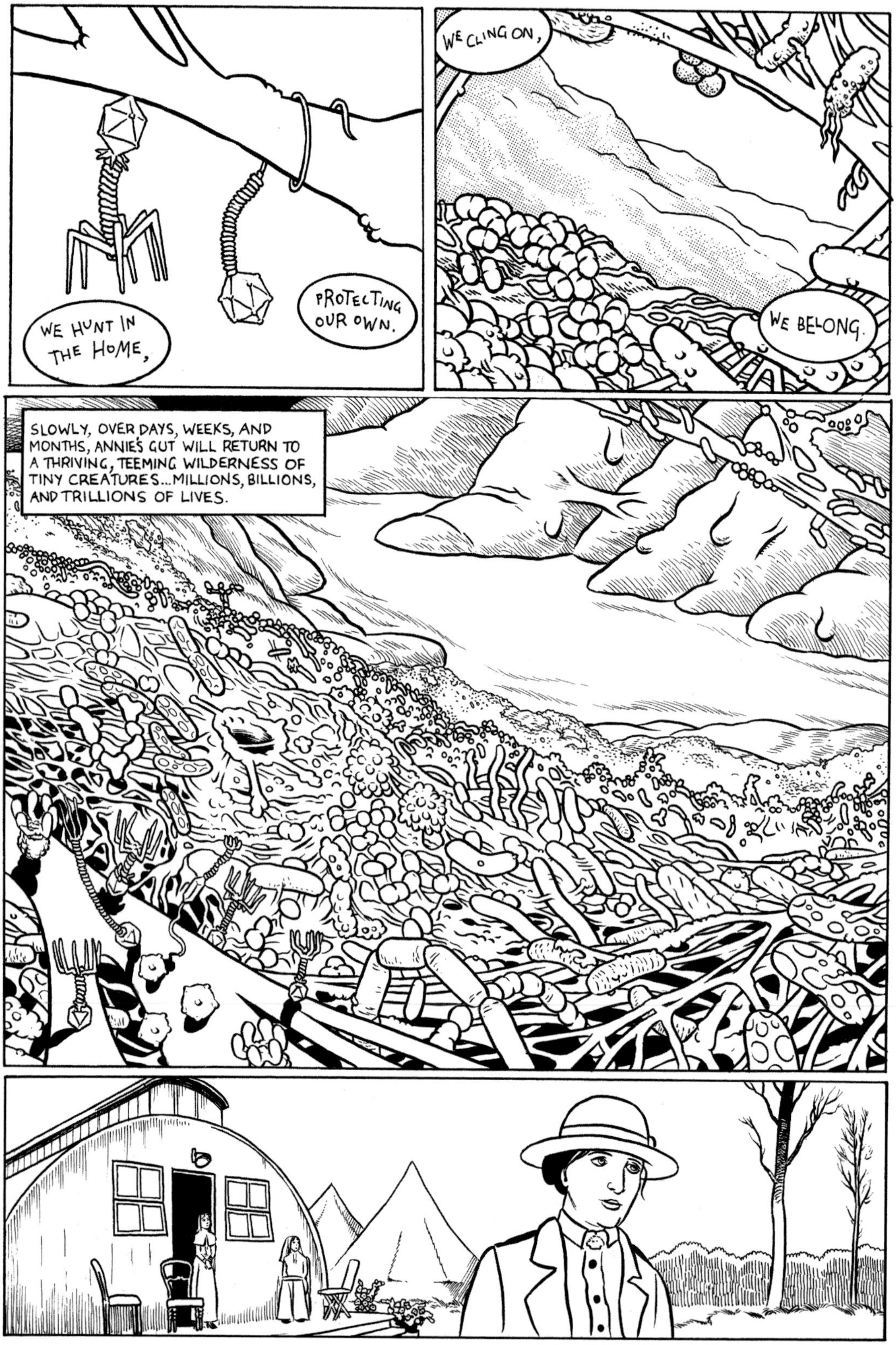
WE HUNT IN THE HOME,
PROTECTING OUR OWN.
WE CLING ON,
WE BELONG.
SLOWLY, OVER DAYS, WEEKS, AND MONTHS, ANNIE'S GUT WILL RETURN TO A THRIVING, TEEMING WILDERNESS OF TINY CREATURES...MILLIONS, BILLIONS, AND TRILLIONS OF LIVES.

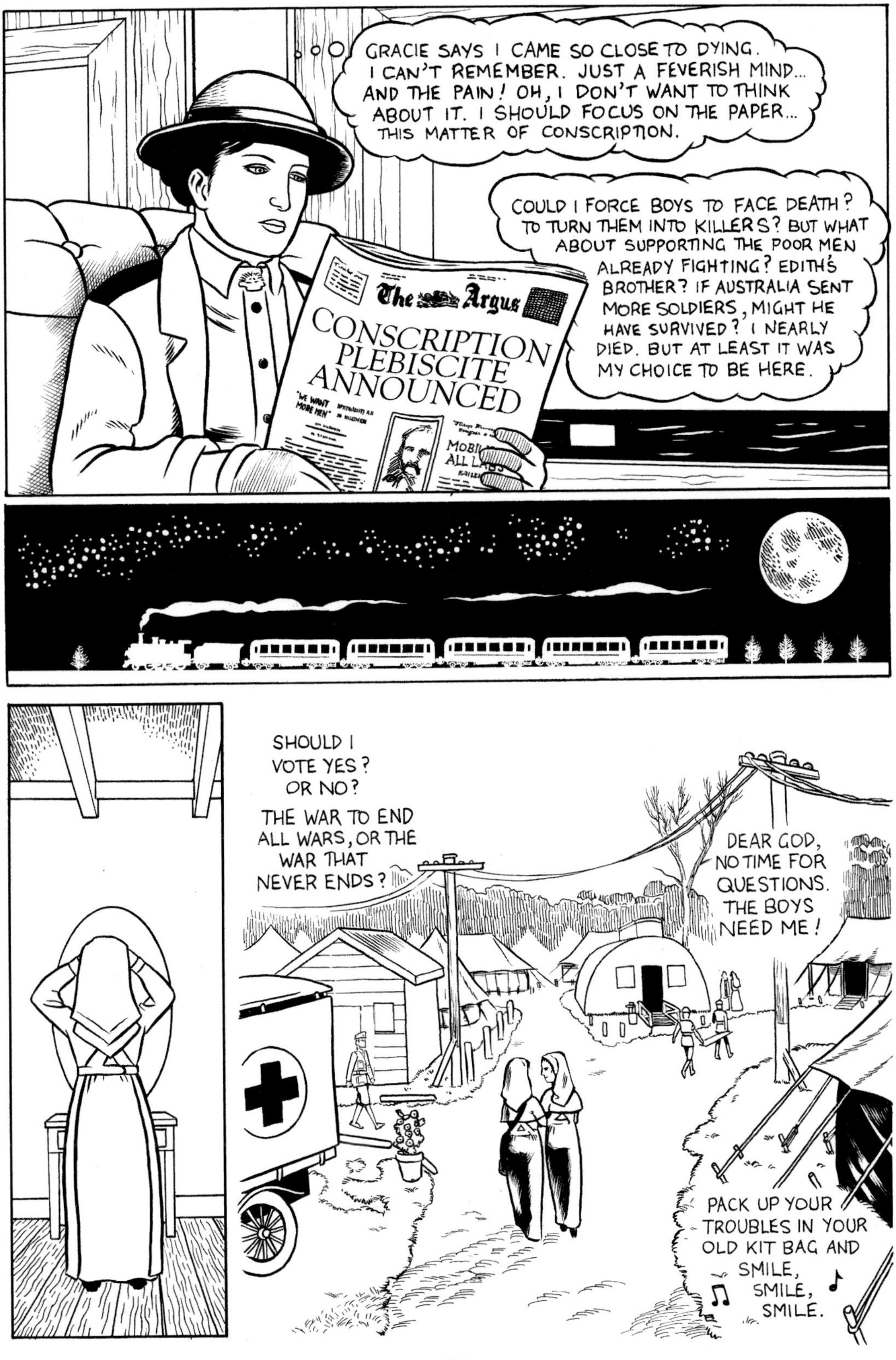
GRACIE SAYS I CAME SO CLOSE TO DYING. I CAN'T REMEMBER. JUST A FEVERISH MIND... AND THE PAIN! OH, I DON'T WANT TO THINK ABOUT IT. I SHOULD FOCUS ON THE PAPER... THIS MATTER OF CONSCRIPTION.
COULD I FORCE BOYS TO FACE DEATH? TO TURN THEM INTO KILLERS? BUT WHAT ABOUT SUPPORTING THE POOR MEN ALREADY FIGHTING? EDITH'S BROTHER? IF AUSTRALIA SENT MORE SOLDIERS, MIGHT HE HAVE SURVIVED? I NEARLY DIED. BUT AT LEAST IT WAS MY CHOICE TO BE HERE.
The Argus
CONSCRIPTION PLEBISCITE ANNOUNCED
"WE WANT MORE MEN"
SHOULD I VOTE YES? OR NO?
THE WAR TO END ALL WARS, OR THE WAR THAT NEVER ENDS?
DEAR GOD, NO TIME FOR QUESTIONS. THE BOYS NEED ME!
PACK UP YOUR TROUBLES IN YOUR OLD KIT BAG AND SMILE, SMILE, SMILE.

THE INVISIBLE WAR: BIG TO SMALL

Miles/Kilometers miles/km

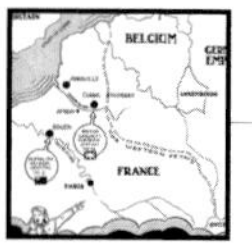
BELGIUM
FRANCE

932 miles (1,500 km) from the North Sea to Switzerland

The western front

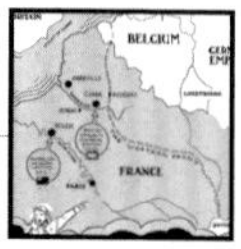
BELGIUM
FRANCE

590 miles (950 km) east to west

France

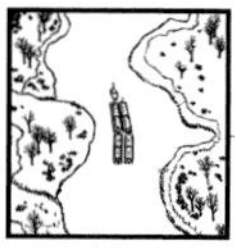

152 miles (245 km) long

The Somme River

mi

Feet/Meters ft/m

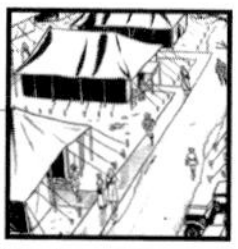

656 feet (200 m) wide

Casualty Clearing Station

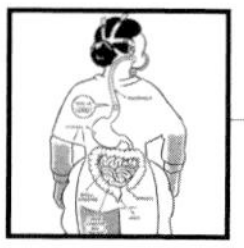

29.5 feet (9 m) long

The human digestive system

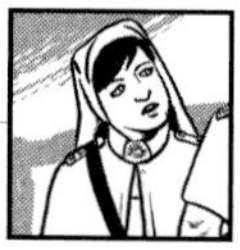

5.2 feet (1.58 m) tall

Annie

ft

Inches/ Millimeters (in/mm)

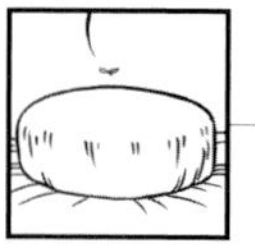

4.7 inches (120 mm) tall

Wheel of Camembert

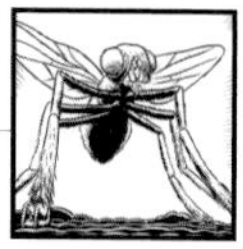

0.3 inches (8 mm) long

Fly

in

Micrometers

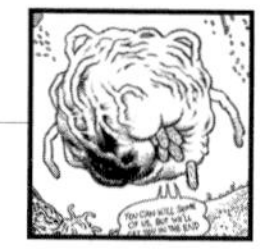

15 μm

White blood cells (neutrophil)

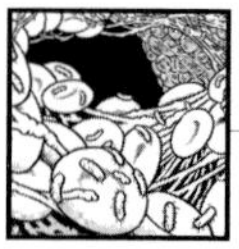

8 μm

Red blood cells

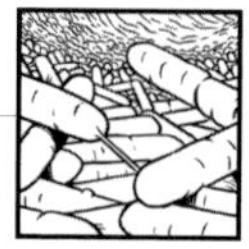

5 μm

Bacteroides (bacteria)

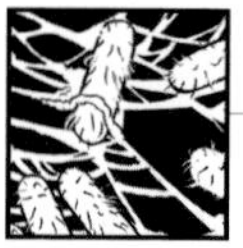

3 μm

Shigella flexneri (bacteria)

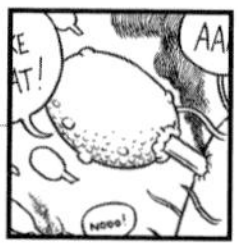

1 μm

Prevotella (bacteria)

μm

Nanometers

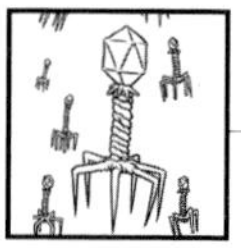

200 nm

Myophage (virus)

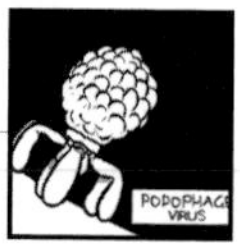

100 nm

Podophage (virus)

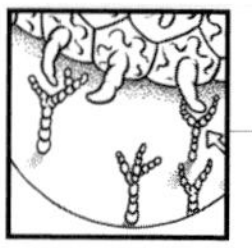

10 nm wide

Glycan branch (mucus)

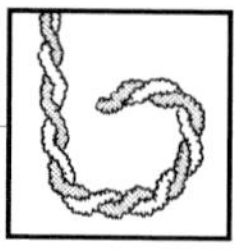

2 nm wide

DNA (deoxyribonucleic acid)

nm

Picometers

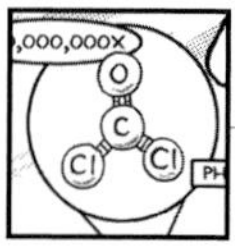
O
C
Cl
Cl

150 pm

Phosgene ($COCl_2$)

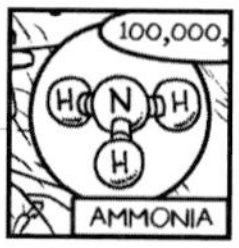
100,000,
H
N
H
H
AMMONIA

70 pm

Ammonia (NH_3)

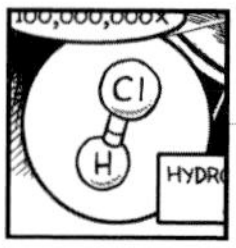
Cl
H

50 pm

Hydrochloric acid (HCl)

pm

THE INVISIBLE WAR Q&A

Where Was the Western Front?
Seen on page 4

The western front was the main theater of war during World War I. It covered a series of trenches across 932 miles (1,500 km) of Europe, from the North Sea across Belgium and France to the border of Switzerland.

What Is a Casualty Clearing Station?
Seen on page 5

A casualty clearing station is a military medical facility behind (but close to) the front line. They were usually out of reach of artillery fire, but not always! They were sometimes in range of gas attacks—depending on the way the wind blew—and enemy planes often bombed them from the air. These stations did not treat patients long term. They were for initial medical treatment that couldn't be handled closer to the front or as a stop on the way to larger hospitals. The clearing station in the story is British Casualty Clearing Station 21. We chose it because it was a busy place in August 1916.

Who Are the Nurses?
Seen on page 6

Nurses, including the Australian nurses of *The Invisible War*, joined the war effort for similar reasons men did: adventure, patriotism, and a desire to see the world. They

also went to be closer to their brothers and friends. Their work was hard and dirty. It included lifting heavy patients and dealing with blood, pus, and excrement. Wartime nurses lived under strict military discipline. Women were only allowed to serve as nurses in the Australian military if they were not married or were widowed. They were also required to have a high standard of moral behavior.

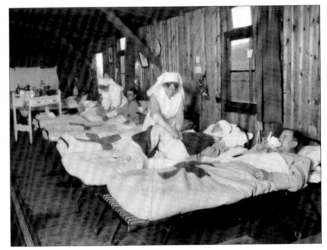

Image: No.2 Australian CCS at Trois Arbres 1917.
Source: Historic Collection/Alamy Stock Photo

Who Are the Patients?

Seen on page 6

Along the western front and elsewhere, shells, bullets, and hand-to-hand bayonet fighting blew holes in men, ruptured their skin, destroyed organs, and tore off limbs. Soldiers would then arrive at the casualty clearing station by field ambulance. Nurses' caseloads included surgical patients treated for shrapnel removal and amputations. Gangrene and harm caused by poison gas were also common. Stress, lack of nutrition, and poor hygiene meant nurses were also working with large numbers of sick and diseased soldiers.

Rations for soldiers were poor, lacking in fresh food. Combat continually interrupted soldiers' sleep. There were times when soldiers could not access clean water and the only available drinking water was rainwater collected from shell holes. These holes might have had blown-apart human or animal corpses in them. Shell-hole water, polluted by a corpse, was commonly known as ANZAC (Australian and New Zealand Army Corps) soup.

Image: An injured soldier being treated in a trench.
Source: Wellcome Library, London.

What Is Dysentery?

Seen on page 7

Dysentery is a disease of the human intestine that causes bloody diarrhea. Widespread infection of the intestinal wall typically leads to ulceration, loss of blood, the production of massive amounts of mucus—resulting in catastrophic loss of fluid from the human body—and often death. A few different types of dysentery exist, but the two most important types during World War I were amebic dysentery and bacillary dysentery. Bacillary dysentery (or shigellosis)—seen in *The Invisible War*—is named after the bacillus (or rod-shaped) bacteria from the genus *Shigella*.

There are four different species of *Shigella*: *dysenteriae, flexneri, sonnei,* and *boydii. Shigella flexneri* and *S. dysenteriae* were the most problematic of these in the trenches of World War I. At this time, the name Shiga was used to describe the bacterium *Shigella dysenteriae*, while *Shigella flexneri* were referred to as Flexner. It wasn't until the 1950s that the different species were united within the same genus.

All species of *Shigella* call human intestines home but cause slightly different forms of dysentery. Dysentery is still a common disease among many communities around the world, particularly in Asia and Africa, where more than two billion people live without regular access to clean drinking water and toilets. Antibiotic-resistant *Shigella* are also making a comeback, with outbreaks in countries such as the United States.

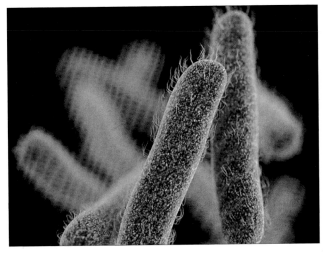

Image: Digital illustration of *Shigella* bacteria.
Source: James Archer, US Centers for Disease Control and Prevention.

Why Do the Shiga Leave Private Robbins's Gut?
Seen on page 10

Once the *Shigella* begin to infect the epithelial cells lining the human intestine, their numbers explode exponentially—from tens to thousands to millions to billions within twenty-four to forty-eight hours! In response, the human intestine makes several liters of mucus in an attempt to flush out as many *Shigella* as possible. This means that most *Shigella* bacteria don't really leave their host intestine by choice. Rather, they are forced out. But there is always a small chance the *Shigella* might find their way onto food or into drinking water and then colonize new human hosts. (The slime the *Shigella* refer to is the mucus made by specialized human epithelial cells—called goblet cells—in the large intestine.)

What's So Important about a Stool Sample?
Seen on page 13

During World War I, members of the Australian medical staff, Lieutenant Colonel C. J. Martin and Sister F. E. Williams, developed some tools for diagnosing dysentery. Most people would have used a combination of tests to diagnose a suspected case: direct observation of the size and shape of the bacteria under a microscope, spreading bacteria from the stool sample on an agar plate that only allowed *Shigella* bacteria to grow, and a serum analysis that exposed a patient's stool sample to a mixture of different antibodies. The serum analysis was the most accurate test available to doctors at the time. If the stool contained *Shigella flexneri*, antibodies would recognize and bind to the bacteria, forming visible clumps in the test tube. That patient was then considered positive for *Shigella flexneri*.

These were very new diagnostic tools at the time. In the early 1900s, an understanding of microbes and microbiology was still limited. World War I was fought without antibiotics, and many soldiers died from bacterial infections resulting from small wounds and scratches. Diagnosis was also a subject of conflict. Some doctors were reluctant to accept new methods for diagnosis and, instead, preferred to trust their old tools: observation and experience. The doctor in *The Invisible War* represents those who were afraid of the new diagnostic tools. But by the end of the war, bacteriology (or microbiology) had become firmly established as a respected tool of medicine.

What Does the Matron Mean by "Down the Line"?
Seen on page 16

"Down the line" means "away from the front, through military channels." (And "up the line" means "towards the front.") The flow chart at right shows how the sick and injured were transported "down the line" and the various stops along the way.

Where Are the Shiga Gang Going inside of Annie?
Seen on pages 20–22

The Shiga gang are aiming to infect Annie's gut. But first, they enter Annie's digestive system through her mouth. The job of the human digestive system is to break down food into small bits that can be absorbed to make energy and new cells for our bodies. The gastrointestinal tract runs from our mouth through the stomach, small intestine, and large intestine, ending at the anus. A type of internal skin called the epithelium lines the gastrointestinal tract and creates a protective layer of mucus. The gastrointestinal tract is about 23 to 33 feet (7 to 10 m) long in an adult human.

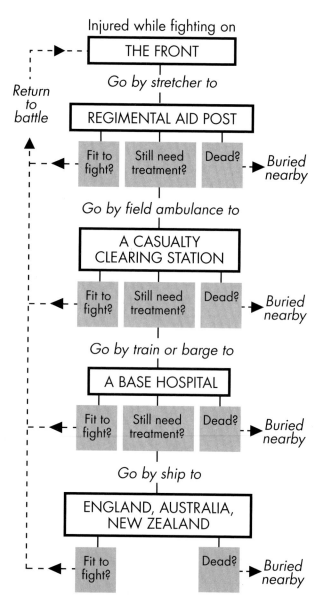

Injured while fighting on
THE FRONT
Go by stretcher to
REGIMENTAL AID POST

| Fit to fight? | Still need treatment? | Dead? |

Buried nearby

Return to battle

Go by field ambulance to
A CASUALTY CLEARING STATION

| Fit to fight? | Still need treatment? | Dead? |

Buried nearby

Go by train or barge to
A BASE HOSPITAL

| Fit to fight? | Still need treatment? | Dead? |

Buried nearby

Go by ship to
ENGLAND, AUSTRALIA, NEW ZEALAND

| Fit to fight? | | Dead? |

Buried nearby

When the *Shigella* bacteria enter Annie's mouth, they encounter a mix of the food and drink she consumed, freshly secreted saliva, and her mouth's resident bacteria and viruses. A human mouth makes about 1 quart (1 L) of saliva each day, mostly to help with chewing but also to begin breaking apart the chemical bonds holding the food molecules together. Human saliva also contains the enzyme known as lysozyme. This enzyme can kill many pathogenic (disease-causing) bacteria threatening to invade our bodies—but unfortunately not the invading *Shigella* bacteria.

Inside the stomach, both physical and chemical processes break food into smaller and smaller particles—allowing the body to absorb many of the tiny molecules, such as glucose, through the stomach wall and into a person's bloodstream. The stomach's highly acidic conditions are dangerous for the bacteria. The regular release of hydrochloric acid (HCl) into the digestive juices of the stomach helps to break apart many of the food molecules for easier absorption. It also kills many bacteria hitching a ride on any swallowed pieces of food.

Why Are the Shiga Gang Going So Fast Down the Small Intestine? And What Is the Bile Waterfall?
Seen on page 25

The entry of food into the small intestine triggers the release of a digestive juice called bile. Bile flows from the gall bladder. It contains enzymes that help break down food and salts that help mop up healthy fat particles for absorption into the body. Together with the mucus lining the small intestine, bile also helps to lubricate the continuous movement of all food particles, along with any bacteria, further downstream. Tiny fingerlike clusters of cells called microvilli coat the 13 to 16 feet (4 to 5 m) of small intestine and help it absorb food particles. If flattened out, the surface area of the microvilli would add up to about 323 square feet (30 sq. m)—the size of a large room.

Why Are There So Many Bacteria in the Gut?
Seen on page 27

Microbiologists estimate that ten to one hundred trillion bacteria live in and on the human body. Most of these live inside the large intestine (often called the gut, or colon). These bacteria are responsible for breaking down anything the mouth, stomach, or small intestine hasn't previously broken down. The two most common types of bacteria in the gut are from the genus *Prevotella* and genus *Bacteroides* (Tella and Roidey in our story). In return for a home and a supply of food, these and other bacteria create and release nutrients for their human host, such as calcium, vitamins B1/B2/B12/K, and hormones such as serotonin.

But Aren't Bacteria Bad?

Seen on page 27

While bacteria such as *Shigella* and *Salmonella* are parasites, causing harm to their host, most microbes in the gut are beneficial. They create valuable vitamins, nutrients, and hormones. Even harmful or parasitic microbes can help train a person's immune system, leading to a lower level of autoimmune diseases. The type of food and how much we eat can be a matter of life and death for many of the microbes in our gut. The inability to digest food or water during a bout of dysentery could ultimately mean death for both microbes and their host.

The microbes in the gut mostly cooperate, much like they would in a compost heap—recycling everything. The waste product of one type of bacteria is the foodstuff for another type of bacteria, creating a sea of possible ingredients to swap and share. But it's not all happy times and cooperation, because many microbes compete for food and space. In fact, one major role of our resident gut bacteria is to take up space in and on the mucus. This prevents harmful bacteria from gaining a foothold and causing disease.

Who Are the Phage Swarm?

Seen on page 29

Bacteriophage (or phage) are types of viruses that infect bacteria. The name comes from two parts: *bacteria* and the Greek word *phagein* (to eat). It literally means bacterial eaters. Bacteriophage are the most numerous biological entity on the planet. There are an estimated 10^{31} phage on Earth. That's a one with 31 zeroes after it. It's more than the number of stars in the observed universe. If you stacked all the phage on Earth end to end, the stack would go about one hundred million light-years!

And what's a virus? Viruses are small DNA- or RNA-based life-forms. They typically range in size from 7.9e-7 to 1.2e-5 inches (20 to 300 nm). Viruses need to infect a host cell in order to replicate. They have been found to infect all types of cellular life-forms on Earth. This makes viruses the most successful predators on the planet.

Common viruses of humans include influenza, herpes, gastroenteritis, HIV, chicken pox, the hepatitis viruses, and the common cold. Viruses also cause more rare infections, such as rabies, Ebola, SARS, and polio. However, not all viruses are bad. Bacteriophage are nature's most successful predators of bacteria. So many scientists consider them to be beneficial to their hosts.

Unlike almost all other forms of life, viruses do not breathe. Nor do they carry many of the genes or parts to perform the chemical reactions typically associated with being alive. While some scientists describe viruses as being "at the edge of life," many do consider viruses to be alive, due to their ability to replicate and evolve. Viruses also possess an ability to make decisions and adapt to changing situations, just like cellular life-forms.

What Are the Different Types of Bacteriophage?

Seen on page 29

Virologists usually group different types of bacteriophage based on size, shape, and other physical traits. The group Caudovirales are bacteriophage that contain tails. Caudovirales includes Myophage, which have a space-lander shape; Siphophage, which have a long siphon or cylinder-shaped tail; and Podophage, which have a very short or footlike tail. Other phage types, such as the Cystophage, don't have tails.

Most of the viruses found in nature are assembled by the repeated connection of a few types of proteins. These repeated connections typically create viruses with the symmetrical form of a helix or an icosahedron (twenty-sided shape). But many bacteriophage carry both an icosahedron head and a helix tail. They are remarkable for their robotic shapes and patterns.

What Is This Lock Thing?

Seen on page 31

Like all viruses, bacteriophage need to get inside their specific host cell before they can replicate. To do this, they must first attach to specific receptors on the surface of the cell. Receptors on the surface of bacteria (such as proteins or lipopolysaccharides) are usually specific to that type of bacteria, so bacteriophage have to create attachment proteins to fit the precise shape of these surface receptors, much like fitting a key into a lock.

Once the bacteriophage key successfully locks onto the surface protein of a bacterium, the infection process begins. Some viruses, disguised as a food molecule, will trick their host into swallowing them through the host's cell wall and membrane. But most bacteriophage will instead puncture a hole in the bacterial cell wall and cell membrane, then deliver their DNA or RNA genome through their tail and into the cell—leaving an empty phage shell behind on the surface of the cell.

How Do Phage Kill Bacteria?

Seen on page 32

Once a virus or viral genome enters a cell, it will try to take control of the host machinery. Sometimes the bacterial host defenses succeed in critically damaging or destroying the invading virus genome, by using DNA-cutting enzymes. But viruses are small and fast, adapting quickly to new challenges.

A virus replicates from one to one hundred in twenty minutes. And within a matter of seconds after injection, the virus genes initiate a counterattack to silence host bacterial defenses. Next, the virus genome forms into a circle to begin making new copies using host DNA (replication). Structural proteins are made next, using amino acids from the host to build new bacteriophage "shells." New virus components (both proteins and the genome) are assembled into dozens of new complete bacteriophage. Finally, the phage produce a mixture of two killer enzymes—a holin and a lysin. Holins form a hole in the bacterial membrane, which then lets the lysin enzymes chew through the bacterial cell wall. Both enzymes cause the bacteria to burst, releasing dozens of new bacteriophage into the surrounding liquid.

Instead of killing their host bacterium, sometimes bacteriophage will choose to insert their DNA into the host bacterial genome. There, the phage can sit and wait while their genome is automatically copied each time the host bacterial cell divides in half to create two new daughter cells. Amazingly, the phage DNA can often sense when the host bacterium is under stress (e.g., starvation) and withdraw from the host genome. This triggers a cycle in which dozens of new copies of the phage assemble and burst from their host.

How Do the Phage Hunt?

Seen on pages 30 and 33

The phage in our story cover the mucus layer of Annie's gut, waiting to latch onto and infect passing bacteria. To explain how phage adhere to mucus, protecting these surfaces and their animal hosts from invading bacteria, researcher Dr. Jeremy Barr proposed the Bacteriophage Adherence to Mucus (BAM) model. In this scientific model (*below*), the phage heads are covered in tiny proteins that function like hooks, which phage use to grab hold of branches within the mucus layer—much like the loops and hooks of Velcro. By hooking onto the branches, the phage are able to slow down their drifting through the watery mucus layer, allowing them to hunt more successfully for bacteria.

2) Bacteriophage hook onto carbohydrate branches of mucus (mucin) using their Hoc surface proteins.
Bacteriophage
Bacterium
5) Bacteriophage and bacteria are released from epithelium region with new eruptions of mucus.
Hoc surface proteins
Carbohydrate (glycan) branches
Mucin strand within mucus
3) Bacteriophage attach to and infect suitable passing bacteria.
1) Goblet cells secrete mucus from epithelium.
4) More and more bacteriophage are released into mucus, further increasing their chance of infecting bacteria.
Mucus
Goblet cell
Goblet cell
Goblet cell
Epithelium (cell layer)

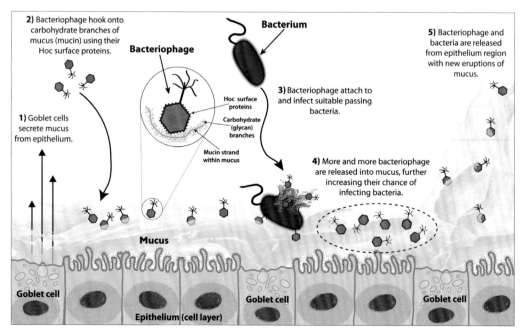

The BAM model can be considered a beneficial symbiosis. The animal producing the mucus benefits from an added protection of bacteriophage, while the bacteriophage benefit from extra opportunities to infect more bacteria, thereby reproducing more often and producing more copies of themselves. Some scientists have gone so far as to describe this as another type of immune system within our bodies, protecting our bodies from being invaded and overrun by any potentially nasty bacteria.

Why Are the Shiga Gang So Happy They Found Some Slime?
Seen on page 33

The slime the Shiga gang refers to in the story is the mucus that the small and large intestines created. The mucus is a source of food for microbes, and its presence suggests the *Shigella* are near their ideal habitat. So what is mucus anyway? A matrix of microbes and molecules, made mostly of water (90 to 95 percent). Mucus gets its slimy structure from long bottlebrushlike molecules called mucins. Made by goblet cells, mucins cover the epithelium and line the intestine. This molecule has a protein backbone surrounded by carbohydrate branches. The mucus matrix is the perfect place for good bacteria to live in your body. It also acts as a barrier against bad bacteria.

As seen on page 34, the Shiga gang dissolve the mucus. To do this, they release an enzyme that cuts away at the carbohydrate (sugar) molecules attached to the mucus. When released, the carbohydrate molecules can act as an energy source for the *Shigella*. And once much of the protective layer of mucus lining the walls of the intestine has been dissolved, the *Shigella* bacteria can potentially achieve their major goal—to infect the underlying human epithelium cells and reproduce.

How and Why Do *Shigella* Update Their Locks?
Seen on page 36

Many scientists believe that bacteria and their viruses have been engaged in an evolutionary arms race for billions of years. Because bacteria and viruses reproduce rapidly, they are able to evolve rapidly too—much faster than plants or animals. Each time a virus attacks a population of bacteria, a handful of bacterial survivors usually resist infection thanks to a mutation or adaptation. These survivors then reproduce to share or spread their protective trait—until the phage eventually adapts to find a new way to infect. One strategy bacteria use to survive bacteriophage infection is to occasionally change their surface receptors. Even a subtle change to the shape of this "lock" can block the virus's "key" from attaching and infecting.

So how did the heroic phage finally have the right key, as seen on page 58? It's a mutant! To adapt to new surface receptors, bacteriophage allow for chance mutations when copying their genes during replication. Even tiny mutations to the phage genes can cause significant changes to the binding proteins (keys) in their tails, creating the possibility of binding to the new surface receptors of bacteria. This ability to adapt can mean the difference between life and death for the bacteriophage and for their human host.

Why Does the Gut Epithelium Cell Let a *Shigella* Bacterium Inside?
Seen on page 41

The *Shigella* bacterium tricks the epithelial cell into swallowing it. It does so by injecting a signal molecule that hijacks the cell's machinery, causing it to open. The epithelial cell then contracts, engulfing the *Shigella*. Once inside, the *Shigella* is able to multiply rapidly and travel sideways into neighboring epithelial cells.

Once the epithelial cell recognizes the *Shigella* bacterium as a foreign invader, it attempts to save the surrounding cells and the body, activating a programmed death sequence designed to kill itself and everything inside it (as seen on page 42). But *Shigella* bacteria can release a molecule to deactivate the programmed cell death sequence. We chose to introduce a kill switch molecule to simplify this very complex process.

What Are Neutrophils?
Seen on page 44

The infection of the gut epithelium by *Shigella* bacteria triggers the release of alarm molecules—which then activate a response from the immune system. The first line of defense against *Shigella* is the release of a type of white blood cell called neutrophil.

Neutrophils migrate from the bloodstream to the site of infection, where they can directly engulf and degrade the bacteria. In an extreme situation, the neutrophils can create neutrophil extracellular traps (NETs). This is a form of self-destruction in which the release of massive amounts of deadly chemicals kills the neutrophils—and many surrounding bacteria.

What Are Those Volcanoes?
Seen on page 46

When under attack from an invasion of pathogenic microbes such as *Shigella* bacteria, the goblet cells in the human intestinal wall will regularly erupt with mucus to flush out the pathogen. But this flushing response requires several liters of water each day. If the flushing action of the gut doesn't quickly succeed in removing the invading cells, its host will eventually risk death from dehydration (loss of water).

What Does the Blood in Annie's Diarrhea Mean?

Seen on page 53

The presence of blood in Annie's stool means she has an infection in her gut. Based on Annie's experience treating Private Robbins, she correctly suspects that she also has dysentery. The epithelium lining of the gut is only one cell thick, with blood capillaries sitting directly underneath. Each time clusters of *Shigella* burst through the epithelium, they break capillaries. Blood then flows into the gut and downstream into the stool.

Why Did the Hospital Use Those Unusual Cures?

Seen on page 56

At the time of World War I, brandy was thought to warm peple up, calm nerves, and ease pain. It would have had negative effects on the body, but nothing too major when dispensed in moderation. Lister's Antidysenteric Serum was created by the Lister Institute, a British research institute working on preventive medicine. The serum was prepared in a horse. Researchers first injected the horse with *Shigella dysenteriae* and *S. flexneri*. The horse's immune system created antibodies in response. These antibodies were thought to help the human immune system mount an attack against infecting *Shigella* and were injected into patients.

Magnesium sulfate and sodium sulfate were both used to induce vomit, but vomiting wouldn't have effectively removed the *Shigella* bacteria from the gut. Induced vomiting may in fact have been harmful. Dysentery patients would already have been losing fluids and were at risk for fatal dehydration. Losing more fluid through vomit would just add to this problem.

As for the hospital itself, nurses who became ill during service were treated in their own wards. It was considered inappropriate to treat them alongside soldiers or civilians. There was a Sick Sister's Ward attached to the 8th British General Hospital in Rouen, France, for this purpose. There were also convalescent homes farther from the front if nurses required a longer recovery time.

ABOUT THE AUTHORS

Briony Barr is a conceptual artist who regularly collaborates with scientists. Her artworks draw on complex systems and microscopic worlds. She is cofounder of Scale Free Network, an art-science collaborative and publisher based in Melbourne, Australia.

Briony Barr

Dr. Gregory Crocetti worked for a decade as a microbial ecologist before cofounding Scale Free Network. His goal is to teach the world that microbes are marvelous.

Gregory Crocetti

Ailsa Wild is a performer, artist, and the author of *The Squid, the Vibrio & the Moon*; *Zobi and the Zoox*; and the Squishy Taylor series. *The Invisible War* is her first graphic novel.

Ailsa Wild

Ben Hutchings has been drawing comics since the early nineties. His work appears all over, from political comics site *The Nib* to the Australian edition of *Mad*, from children's comics to magazines for prison inmates. Ben was a cofounder of Australia's first cartoonists' studio, Squishface Comic Studio, where he works as a freelance cartoonist.

Ben Hutchings

Dr. Jeremy Barr served as the science adviser on *The Invisible War* and is also a lecturer at Monash University's School of Biological Sciences in Melbourne. He is an avid collector of phages and is solely responsible for the lysis and death of trillions of bacteria (all in the name of science, of course).

Jeremy Barr

Created by *Briony Barr & Gregory Crocetti*
Written by *Ailsa Wild*
In collaboration with *Jeremy Barr*, whose research inspired the project.
Illustrated by *Ben Hutchings*
Art direction by *Briony Barr*
Graphic design of Australian edition by *Jaye Carcary*
Science direction by *Gregory Crocetti*
Science research and writing by *Gregory Crocetti*
History research and writing by *Ailsa Wild*
Additional editing by *Beth Askham*
Additional scientific consultation by *François-Xavier Weill, Philippe Sansonetti, Laurent Debarbieux, Kathryn Holt*, and *Merry Youle*
History consultation by *Kirsty Harris*

Jaye Carcary